Widespread Black Boots Were Planted Mere Inches From Her Face.

Her gaze climbed a virile, masculine body packed into denim so tight, the cloth looked painted on. He had a lean waist, a shapely torso and a linebacker's squared-off wide shoulders. A bright halo backlit a well-shaped ebony head.

She couldn't see the fierce face that went with this diabolical individual, but his bold, stripping gaze made her shiver.

Was this oversexed caveman with the massive biceps a figment of her maddeningly fertile imagination? She shut her eyes, and when she opened them, the scuffed black boots were an inch closer.

"Do you know how to say thank you?"

His blazing eyes settled on her face, moved lower with an overabundance of feral sensuality. And when he wrapped his arms around her in the darkness, when he touched her, she got the sexual charge she'd been waiting for her whole life.

From him.

She was too shocked to resist as his fingers on her skin just got hotter and hotter.

Instantaneous man-woman combustion.

Dear Reader,

This Fourth of July, join in the fireworks of Silhouette's 20th anniversary year by reading all six powerful, passionate, provocative love stories from Silhouette Desire!

July's MAN OF THE MONTH is a *Bachelor Doctor* by Barbara Boswell. Sparks ignite when a dedicated doctor discovers his passion for his loyal nurse!

With *Midnight Fantasy,* beloved author Ann Major launches an exciting new promotion in Desire called BODY & SOUL. Our BODY & SOUL books are among the most sensuous and emotionally intense you'll ever read. Every woman wants to be loved…BODY & SOUL, and in these books you'll find a heady combination of breathtaking love and tumultuous desire.

Amy J. Fetzer continues her popular WIFE, INC. miniseries with *Wife for Hire.* Enjoy *Ride a Wild Heart,* the first sexy installment of Peggy Moreland's miniseries TEXAS GROOMS. This month, Desire offers you a terrific two-books-in-one value—*Blood Brothers* by Anne McAllister and Lucy Gordon. A British lord and an American cowboy are look-alike cousins who switch lives temporarily…and lose their hearts for good in this romance equivalent of a doubleheader. And don't miss the debut of Kristi Gold, with her moving love story *Cowboy for Keeps*—it's a keeper!

So make your summer sizzle—treat yourself to all six of these sultry Desire romances!

Happy Reading!

Joan Marlow Golan

Joan Marlow Golan
Senior Editor, Silhouette Desire

Please address questions and book requests to:
Silhouette Reader Service
U.S.: 3010 Walden Ave., P.O. Box 1325, Buffalo, NY 14269
Canadian: P.O. Box 609, Fort Erie, Ont. L2A 5X3

Midnight Fantasy
ANN MAJOR

Silhouette®
Desire.
Published by Silhouette Books
America's Publisher of Contemporary Romance

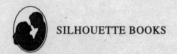 SILHOUETTE BOOKS

ISBN 0-373-76304-2

MIDNIGHT FANTASY

Copyright © 2000 by Ann Major

This edition published by arrangement with Harlequin Books S.A.

® and TM are trademarks of Harlequin Books S.A., used under license.
Trademarks indicated with ® are registered in the United States Patent
and Trademark Office, the Canadian Trade Marks Office and in other
countries.

Visit Silhouette at www.eHarlequin.com

Printed in U.S.A.

Books by Ann Major

ANN MAJOR

loves writing romance novels as much as she loves reading them. She is a proud mother of three children, who are now in college. She lists hiking in the Colorado mountains with her husband, playing tennis, sailing, enjoying her cats and playing the piano among her favorite activities. Be sure to look for her next release, *Wild Enough for Willa*, in December 2000 from MIRA Books.

To Aaron Clark, my late cousin, and his widow,
Glenda Clark. There are lessons in life,
both dark and bright. Sometimes the dark ones teach us
what we most need to know.

Aaron, you have blazed bright with love.
You have taught me about courage. You have taught me
that it is never too late to begin anew. You have become
everything and more than you ever dreamed.
You are one of my real-life heroes.

To Glenda, who taught me more about real love
than almost anyone I know.

Prologue

Get the hell out of here, you half-wild, no-good bastard!

The van swerved off the asphalt. A rumble of bumps and rattles jolted the prisoner on the floorboards back to queasy consciousness. Murky, gray light filtered through his blindfold.

He saw his father's face, mottled with rage.

You're damn sure no son of mine!

He'd turned away, knowing what he'd always felt deep down, that he was nothing. He'd gotten his start in the gutter. That's where he should have stayed.

The stench of dank air made him shudder.

God, he was scared. So scared.

They were in the swamp now, in that eerie, primeval kingdom of cypress trees, stagnant brown bayous, knobby-headed gators and mud deep enough to swallow a man whole.

Cajun music whined through bursts of static. He was

bound hand and foot, sprawled on top of smelly fast-food boxes, Styrofoam cups and candy wrappers.

The waxy-faced driver with the spider tattoo was driving faster than he had in New Orleans. "You're gonna be gator food, boy."

A surge of fresh fear shook the captive.

Another voice. "You know what gators do, don't you, no?"

A boot nudged the prisoner's hip. "They'll drag you to some underground hole, stuff you inside, yes, and tear off little bits of you for days."

A *strange terror* gripped the blindfolded man. When he shifted on top of the garbage, something squished against his clean-shaven face. Only yesterday he'd sat with his father in the best restaurant in the French Quarter. He swallowed carefully against the gag, fighting not to choke on the oily rag in his mouth and the coppery flavor of his own blood. He tried not to breathe because every tortured breath made weird, gargling noises in his broken nose.

His assailants' mood was quiet, tense, electric.

The road got bumpier, wetter; the pungent odor of still, dark waters and rotting vegetation stronger.

Big tires sloshed to a standstill.

"Let's dump him. Sack him up, throw those concrete blocks in. Haul him out deep so he sinks."

The back doors were thrown open. His fine Italian loafers came off when they grasped him around the ankles and pulled him roughly over garbage, tools, and bits of wood. They flung him onto the muddy ground, and his head struck a rotten log. When he regained consciousness, they were waist deep, pushing him under.

He fought to stand up in the gummy mud, but a boot sent him reeling in the warm, soupy water. Panic surged through him when big hands clamped around his shoulders and pressed him deeper.

He fought. His lungs burned with the fierce will to breathe. He pushed harder and was stunned when their grip on his neck miraculously loosened. His head broke the surface, and he choked on watery breaths as a shell was racked into a chamber. A shotgun blast exploded. Then everything got quiet.

He reeled backwards, flopping helplessly as the weights pulled him under. Strangely, as he began to sink, dying, his terror subsided.

All was peace and darkness.

Was this how she'd felt when her alarm went off and she couldn't get up?

Again he was a frightened, guilt-stricken boy shivering in wet pajamas. Bear tucked under his arm, he'd padded into his mother's dark bedroom. Bright sunshine lit her black, tangled hair. Lost in shadows her body was a slovenly heap, half on, half off the bed.

Her alarm kept ringing. He'd lain for hours, listening to that ringing till it had become a roar in his head. She was mean most mornings. Mean every night. How he lived for those rare moments when she tried to be nice, when she read to him from the books Miss Ancil loaned him from the library.

As always her bedroom stank of booze and cigarettes.

"Mommy! I—I's sorry, so sorry…I wet….."

He'd called her name after this confession and promised the way he did every morning never ever to do it again.

Only she hadn't cussed him. Nor had she gathered him into her arms and clung to him as if he were very dear which she sometimes did. She'd just lain there.

Finally, he'd gone to her and shaken her. "Open your eyes. Please, Mommy." He'd touched her cheek. She'd felt so stiff and cold…like his frosted windowpane in winter. Her alarm clock kept ringing.

He hadn't thought of that morning in years. Then here it was, his last thought on earth.

After her funeral his aunts had marched him over to his father's house. A man with black hair and blazing silver eyes had thrown open the door. His aunts had pushed him forward just as the door had slammed.

He'd been shuffled among distant kinfolk who had too many kids of their own. He'd done time in foster homes with other throwaways like himself, gotten in trouble at school. Then, miraculously, his father had had a change of heart and adopted him. He'd done everything in the world to please his father, eventually, even going into business with him.

Then one night he'd worked late and without warning opened the wrong file on a computer.

A gush of water soaked his gag, slid down his throat, up his nostrils, burning, strangling. He was dying when brutal hands manacled his waist, maneuvered his head forcefully to the surface, dragged him out of the water and flung him onto the muddy bank.

A rough voice cursed him in Cajun French. Gnarled fingers tore off his soggy blindfold, ripped at the duct tape over his mouth, then yanked the gag out.

"Jesus." His rescuer's breath stank of gin and tobacco as he pounded his back. Water trickled out of the drowning man's lips in spurts.

"Damn it," he pleaded.

The hard palm froze. "Ha! So! You're alive!"

He was rolled over and a flashlight jammed under his chin. "You don't look too good."

"Damn it!" He grabbed the light and shone it at his rescuer.

The stranger had wrinkled brown skin, white hair, and soulless black eyes. "You don't look so good yourself."

Yellow teeth flashed in an irreverent grin. "The name's

Frenchy.'' Frenchy seized his long black flashlight and turned it off. ''Frenchy LeBlanc. I was just helping my brother check his trotlines. We fell out…. He's kinda cranky.''

''Not like you…sweet as sugarcane.''

With a grin, Frenchy ripped off the tape at the prisoner's ankles along with a wad of dark body hair.

''Ouch!''

''You need a ride home? A hospital? Or the police station?''

''I'm okay.''

''You're beat up pretty bad—'' When he said nothing, Frenchy held out his hand and helped him to his feet. ''You gotta name, boy?''

He hesitated. Then, just like that, a name popped up from his childhood. But his voice sounded rusty when he used it. ''Tag…''

The older man eyed him. ''Tag. Tag what?''

Right. Right. Last name. ''Campbell… Tag…Campbell.''

''Like hell!'' The yellow grin brightened. ''You been to Texas…*Tag?*''

Tag shook his head.

The older man's gaze appraised his tall, muscular body. ''You got soft hands for a big guy…and a hard face…and eyes that don't quite match it. That suit, even trashed, looks like it set you back some.''

Tag said nothing.

''Real work might do you good—''

''Damn it…if you're going to insult me—''

''I fish. I could use a deckhand.''

Tag turned away helplessly, and stared at the lurid shadows the cypress trees with their draperies of moss made. *A deckhand. Minimum wage.* For years he'd been on the fast track. His education. His career. His high-flying plans for his father's company. He'd been good, really really good at one thing.

But he couldn't go back.

"I've always worked in an office, but I lift weights in my gym every afternoon. I've never had time to fish," he said. *Never wanted to.* But he didn't say that.

Frenchy nodded, taking in more than was said. "I don't blame you for saying no to such hard, thankless work."

"I didn't say no, old man.... You'd have to teach me."

Frenchy patted his shoulder. "You gotta job."

"Thanks." Tag's voice was hoarse. He was disgusted that it might betray eagerness and gratitude. He knew better than to believe that this crude stranger or his casual offer and his kindness tonight meant anything.

He was through with ambition, through with dreams, through with false hopes that led nowhere. Again he was staring into his father's cold gray eyes. He was through with family and dreams of real love, too.

A deckhand. A trashy job working for a crude, trashy guy.

Get the hell out of here, you half-wild, no-good bastard.

"Thanks, Frenchy," Tag repeated in a colder, darker tone.

One

Five years later...

Stay with me, Frenchy. I need you.

That's as close as Tag had come to telling the best friend he'd ever had, he loved him.

But maybe Frenchy had known.

Tag had clasped him in his arms long after Frenchy's eyes had gone as glassy as the still bay, long after his skin had grown as cool as his dead mother's that awful morning when the alarm clock had kept ringing.

Stay with me, Frenchy.

He'd lashed the wheel of the shrimp boat to starboard with a nylon sheet...his makeshift autopilot...and headed home, cradling Frenchy's limp, grizzled head in his lap.

Stay with me, Frenchy.

But Frenchy's eyes had remained closed.

The deck had rolled under them.

* * *

It was midnight. The full moon shone through the twisted
live oaks and tall grasses, casting eerie shadows across
Frenchy's tombstone. Tag was all alone in that small, pic-
turesque, historical cemetery located on a mound of higher
earth that overlooked Rockport's moonwashed bay. Come
morning, this time of year, the graves would be ablaze with
wildflowers. Funny, how death could make you see the
truth you didn't want to see. Tag had been living so hard
and fast for so long, he hadn't admitted he'd loved the old
bastard, till he'd held his friend's limp body and begun to
weep.

"This wasn't supposed to happen! Damn your hide,
Frenchy, for leaving me like everybody else…. But most
of all I damn you for making me give a damn. It should
be me who's dead."

They'd buried Frenchy beside his son, the son he'd lost
right before Frenchy had saved Tag's life.

Tag was glad the cemetery was deserted. He didn't want
anybody to see how profoundly Frenchy's death had upset
him.

Sunken black circles ringed Tag's bloodshot eyes; his
jaw was shadowed with several days of dark stubble. His
stomach rumbled painfully from too much liquor and too
little food.

The moon shone high in a cloudless, bright sky. The salt-
laden sea air smelled of dry earth and newly mown grass.
Frenchy's favorite kind of night. The shrimp would be running. Not that Tag could bear the thought of shrimping
under a full moon without Frenchy.

Tag's big black bike was parked a little way from Frenchy's tombstone under a live oak tree that had been
sculpted by the southeasterly prevailing winds that blew off
the gulf, cooling its protected bays and low-lying coastal
prairies.

Tag was kneeling before the pink tombstone. Soft as a prayer, his deep voice whispered. "Haunt me, Frenchy. Damn you, haunt me. Stay with me."

"You don't need an old man past his prime. You need a woman, kids," Frenchy had pointed out, in that maddening know-it-all way of his, a few nights ago.

"Strange advice coming from a man who's failed at marriage four times."

"Nothing like a pretty woman to make a man old enough to know better hope for the best. Life's a circle, constantly repeating itself."

God, I hope not.

"You're young. But you'll get old. You'll die. Life's short. You gotta fall in love, get married, spawn kids, repeat the circle."

"There's places in my circle I don't want to revisit."

"You're not the tough guy you pretend. You're the marrying kind."

"Where'd you get a damn fool notion like that?"

"You're either sulkin' or ragin' mad."

"Which is why you think I'd make a delightful husband."

"You don't fit in here. Your heart's not in bars or fights or gambling...or even in fishing. Or even in getting laid by those rich, wild girls who come to Shorty's looking for a fast tumble in the back seat of their car with a tough guy like you."

"What if I said I like what they do to me? And what if I said I can do without a heart, old man?"

"You're a liar. You got a heart, a big one, whether you want it or not. It's just busted all to pieces same as your pretty, sissy-boy face. Only the right woman can fix what ails you."

"You're getting mighty mushy, old man."

"You think you can stay dead forever?"

The wind drifting through moss and honeysuckle brought the scent of the sea, reminding him of the long hours of brutal work on a shrimp boat. The work numbed him. The beauty of the sea and its wildlife comforted him, made this hellish exile in an alien world somehow more endurable. Just as those women and what they did to him in their cars gave him a taste of what he'd once had, so that he could endure this life. But always after the women left, he felt darker, as if everything that was good in him had been used up. Which was what he wanted. Maybe if they used him long enough, he wouldn't feel anything.

Tag knelt in the soft earth and studied the snapshot of a younger Frenchy framed in cracked plastic in the center of the pink stone.

"You're a coward to run from who you are and what you want, Tag Campbell—a coward, pure and simple."

Tag had sprung out of his chair so fast, he'd knocked it over. "You lowdown, ignorant cuss! Every time you drink, your jaw pops like that loose shutter."

Frenchy laughed. "What's the point of wisdom, if I can't pass it on to a blockhead like you? Life's a circle...."

"Don't start that circle garbage."

Tag had slammed out of the beach house, taken the boat out, stayed gone the rest of the night on that glassy, moonlit sea. He hadn't apologized when he saw Frenchy waiting for him on the dock.

Then Frenchy had collapsed on the boat a few hours later when they were setting their nets.

Guilt swamped Tag. He'd never thanked the old man for anything he'd done.

The wind roared up from the bay, murmuring in the oak trees, mocking Tag as his empty silver eyes studied the grave. It was difficult to imagine the hard-living, advice-giving meddler lying still and quiet, to imagine him inside that box, dead. Emotions built inside Tag—guilt, grief—

but he bottled them, the way he always did when he wasn't driving fast, fighting, chasing women, or drinking.

The dangerous-looking man who knelt at his friend's grave bore little resemblance to the younger man whose life Frenchy had saved in a Louisiana swamp. That man had been elegantly handsome before the beating, his smooth features classically designed, the aquiline nose straight, his trusting silver eyes warm and friendly.

That man was dead. As dead as Frenchy.

The powerfully-built man beside the grave was burned dark from the sun. On the inside his heart had charred an even blacker shade. Fists had smashed and rearranged his once handsome features into a ruggedly-brutal composition. The broken nose had been flattened. There was a narrow, white ridge above one brow. Despite these changes, or perhaps because of them, an aura of violence clung to him. Maybe it was this reckless, outlaw attitude that made him so lethally attractive, at least to women of a certain class. Such women cared little about his inner wounds. They came on strong, wanting nothing from him except to use his body for quick, uncomplicated sex.

His guarded silver eyes beneath black arcing brows missed nothing, trusted no one. Especially not such women—women who made him burn, but left him feeling even colder and lonelier when they were done with him and drove off in their fancy cars to their big houses and safe men.

His muscles were heavy from hard, manual labor. He wore scuffed black cowboy boots, tight jeans, a worn white T-shirt, and a black leather jacket.

Frenchy.

Death triggered deep, primal needs.

Death. Violence. Sex. Somehow they went together.

Alone with his demons, without Frenchy to irritate and distract him, Tag needed a bar fight or a woman—bad. So bad, he almost wished he'd gone to the funeral and wrestled some shrimper for a topless waitress. So bad, he almost wished he was in jail nursing a hellish hangover with the rest of Frenchy's wild bunch.

Instead he'd driven his motorcycle—too fast and over such rough roads, he'd almost rolled. He'd scared himself. Which was a sign that cold as he was in his lonely life, he wasn't ready to end it. When he'd calmed down, he'd come to the cemetery to pay his last respects.

The silvery night was warm and lovely.

Perfect kind of weather to hang out in a cemetery perfumed by wild flowers and glistening with moonlight.

If you could stand cemeteries.

Which Tag couldn't. Any more than he could stand funerals. Especially the funeral of his best friend. Not when his own mood was as brittle and hopeless as the morning his mother had died, as the afternoon his father had slammed the door in his face.

Frenchy's funeral had been a blowout brawl at Shorty's. The cocktail waitresses, even Mabel, had danced topless on the pool tables. Some of the shrimpers had found their dance inspiring, and since there weren't ever enough women to go around in Shorty's, the "funeral" had gotten so wild, two of Frenchy's ex-wives had called the cops who hauled the shrimpers and barmaids to jail.

It had been just the sort of uproar that gave shrimpers and the industry a bad name.

Then Frenchy's will had been read. Everybody really got mad when they found out that, fool that he was, Frenchy had left that black dog, Tag Campbell, everything.

Everything. Boats. Restaurant. Fishhouses. Wharves. Even the beach house which was practically an historic landmark. *Everything.*

Campbell.

That snobby bastard! He didn't even like to fish! Still,

he was the best fisherman any of them had ever seen. Just as he was way too popular with *their* women even though he secretly despised them. The bastard preferred books to beer even though he could drink any one of them under the table. Tag Campbell was too proud and high-and-mighty to hang out with the likes of them at Shorty's. How in the hell had he outsmarted them all—even Frenchy?

Everything was his.

There was lots of angry muttering.

"It isn't right! Frenchy dead on that boat with just that lying Tag Campbell to tell the tale."

"If you ask me, the bastard killed him."

"You heard the coroner. Autopsy report says massive coronary. Says Frenchy smoked and drank too much. Says it's a miracle Frenchy lived as long as he did."

"I say it was murder. Frenchy was fit as a fiddle. Why just two nights ago he was drunker than a skunk dancing on that table with Mabel."

Rusty and Hank, two of the rougher prisoners, deckhands Tag had fired for laziness and pure meanness, vowed that as soon as they got loose, they'd see their friend, Frenchy, avenged.

Frenchy had a lot more money than the shrimpers suspected. The sheriff paid Tag a visit just to tell him he'd be smart to leave town, at least till Rusty and Hank cooled off.

At the sight of the sheriff's car in his drive and Trousers, his Border collie, slinking off to the woods, Tag grimaced. No wonder Trousers was scared. The big man cut an impressive figure in his uniform and silvered sunglasses. He had heavy features, squared-off shoulders, and a big black gun hanging from his thick belt.

Tag had dealt with more than his share of armed bullies in uniforms. The law, they called themselves.

Self-righteous bullies, strutting around in their shiny

boots like they owned the world. They'd boarded his boats, slashed his nets, kicked his ice chests over and swept his catch overboard, fined his captains. No sooner had Sheriff Jeffries slammed his meaty fist against his screen door and bellowed Tag's name, than sweat started trickling under his collar. A lot of his cats scurried under the house or after the cowardly Trousers. Others hunkered low behind pot plants to watch the suspicious character stomping down their breezeway.

"I just let Rusty and Hank out. They're calling you a murderer."

You half-wild, no-good bastard.

His own father had wrongly accused him of embezzlement and grand larceny. Anger burned in Tag's throat, but he smiled as if he didn't give a damn and saluted the man with a whiskey bottle. "You got a warrant—"

"Sometimes, Campbell, the smart thing is to walk away."

Tag stared at his own reflection in the silver glasses and then pushed the door wider. "I ain't runnin'."

The sheriff planted himself on his thick legs and then leaned against the doorway.

"Jeffries, those guys talk big when they're safe in jail, but they're like dogs barking from inside a fence. You let 'em out, and they'll lick my hand like puppies."

"Just a friendly warning, Campbell."

"Thanks, amigo."

Still, Tag had opened a drawer, loaded his automatic and stuffed it in the waistband of his jeans before setting out on his bike alone.

Numbly Tag studied his friend's tombstone. Frenchy had been mighty proud of the pink stone. He'd chosen it himself on a lark five years earlier right after he'd brought Tag home. Frenchy was known for cheating at cards, and had won the plot off one of Rockport's most respectable citizens in a drunken poker game at Shorty's.

"You cheated him," the man's indignant wife had ranted, and the whole town, at least the women, had believed her. "You got him drunk, so you could cheat him."

Now Frenchy was as ashamed of his lack of talent at cards which made cheating a necessity as he was proud of his drinking skills. He might have gallantly returned the plot had she not accused him of cheating.

"We wuz drinking his whiskey, I'll have you know, and I was even drunker than he was, lady," Frenchy had declared almost proudly. "Could be *he* cheated *me*."

The lady sued, but the judge, a poker player, had sided with Frenchy.

Tag studied Frenchy's name and the date of his birth and the single line etched in caps on the bottom of the stone— IT WAS FUN WHILE IT LASTED.

Slowly Tag lowered his gaze. Instead of flowers, a mountain of beer cans and baseball caps were piled high on the mound of clods. Indeed, every baseball cap that had been nailed to the ceiling of Shorty's had been enthusiastically ripped off and reverently placed on his grave.

Tag's eyes stung. Frenchy would've been mighty proud.

Grief tore a hole in Tag's wide chest as he slowly rose and stalked over to his bike. He pulled on his black leather jacket, zipped it. Next came his gloves, his black helmet. Straddling the big black monster, jumping down hard, revving the engine, he made enough noise to wake the dead.

But then maybe that was his intention.

Not that it did any good.

Frenchy wasn't coming back.

Tag roared to the gate, skidding to a stop in a pool of brilliant gold that spilled over him from the streetlight.

He turned and looked back at the cemetery.

Stay with me, Frenchy.

Suddenly, time as Tag knew it did a tailspin. Or maybe the world just turned topsy-turvy. Whatever. The moon got bigger. Then it flattened itself into the shape of a huge pink egg in that inky sky. Stars popped like fireworks. For a second or two Tag felt there really might be a mastermind up there.

Tag got all warm and tingly inside. The wind sped up and the silvery night pulsed bluish-pink. A couple of beer cans came loose from the grave and started to roll straight toward Tag.

He shut his eyes, but the same pulsating, vivid rosy-blue fog swirled behind his eyelids, too. He blinked. Open or shut, the otherworldly, blue-pink radiance pulsed.

After a while, somebody, maybe Frenchy, switched off the pink light, and the moon settled down. The streetlamp came back on, gold and bright as ever. The night beyond was silvery dark. The can didn't stop rolling till it hit the toe of Tag's boot. He picked it up, noticed it was Frenchy's favorite brand. Tag flattened the can, stuffed it in his back pocket.

What the hell had that been about? Had the streetlight malfunctioned? Or was it just him?

As he stared at the moon he felt different somehow, not so tight and morose. The hole in his chest seemed to have closed. And the night, like his future, beckoned with amazing possibilities.

Had Frenchy done this? Had he actually haunted him? Had he given him this strange sensation of peace? Of new opportunities?

Hell no. The grief and the booze he'd drunk earlier, coupled with not eating, was getting to him. He was hallucinating.

He'd better make it a short night, grab a burger and go to bed. Warily, he looked both ways before pulling out.

Two cars zoomed recklessly toward him from his right.

Kids, playing chase. Where the hell was Jeffries when there was real work for a big bully with a gun to do?

Impatiently, Tag waited for the juvenile delinquents to pass.

When he caught that first glimpse of long blond hair, the back of his neck began to tingle. She was a rich tart on the prowl for a cheap thrill.

Happy to oblige, pretty lady.

Then *she* came into clearer focus the way a terrified deer does in your headlight.

He didn't notice the make of her late-model, flashy red sports car. He was too busy noticing her. She looked nervous and scared.

He felt her—deep inside. She touched a raw place he hadn't known was still alive. She made him ache and hurt and crave things he'd thought he'd given up for good. What would it be like to have a woman like her waiting at the door with a smile every night when he came home?

In the space of a microsecond he memorized that pale pampered face; those classy, even features she'd painted with way too much makeup, probably to make herself look older and more sophisticated. Pert, shapely breasts spilled above a low-cut white bodice. The style was overly sophisticated for her, too.

He caught a glimpse of something sparkly around her throat. Diamonds? Rich, too?

He knew her type. She was the kind of woman who wanted her real man to be a money machine but found "nice" men too tame in bed. So, she came looking for a guy like him at Shorty's. He'd gone with plenty to motels. Some preferred backseats of cars, but once they got their kicks, they rearranged their skirts and drove off. They never asked his name, and he always felt depressed and cheapened, less than nothing when they were done with him.

Other men envied him his popularity. What the hell was the matter with him? What did he want really?

He couldn't tear his gaze from this one. With her long blond hair streaming behind her, she looked like an angel riding the wind.

He willed her to look at him, to really see him.

Suddenly she tossed her head toward him. Her eyes grew huge the instant she saw him—as if she were equally fascinated and yet scared, too. Again, he thought her different than the others. He had the strangest feeling that if he stared into her eyes long enough, he would rediscover his own soul—which was a crazy feeling, if ever there was one.

Something dangerous and fatal connected them. Unwanted longings and painful needs bubbled too near the surface. His pulse raced out of control.

How could he feel so much in the space of a few heartbeats? She was a baby, younger than her voluptuous body, while he was far older than his years.

"Do you hold yourself as cheap underneath as all the others, baby?" he growled.

The minx flirtily tooted her horn and sped up. As if she wasn't already driving fast, way too fast.

Her little car careened onto the shoulder, pinging his bike and long, denim-clad legs with gravel, but she regained control. The beat-up sedan behind her raced past Tag in hot pursuit. Gravel sprayed his boots and his bike like bullets. Only he didn't get any hormonal bang from these punks.

Damn. He knew that junk heap. Rusty and Hank. Not kids. Two mean guys who were mad at the world in general and out for vengeance against him tonight. What if they took it out on her?

He'd lied to Jeffries. Those guys were bad news. As bad as the thugs who'd almost killed him in the swamp. After he'd fired them, they'd sprayed paint all over the cars in the parking lot out back of Frenchy's restaurant. Painted the outer walls of the kitchen in purple graffiti.

Correction. *His* restaurant now.

He had a score to settle. A damsel as a trophy only upped the stakes.

Tag whipped his big bike onto the asphalt road, gunned it.

The cars raced north at double the speed limit, flying over the lighted bridge, veering left on screaming tires, onto Fulton Beach Road. The moonlit bay glittered to the east of them. The mansions on pilings that lined the canals loomed tall and dark to the west.

The quaint road along the beach, with its cottages, historic Fulton Mansion and motels, narrowed, roughened, but the girl and her pursuers kept driving like maniacs. Just as she got to the wharves and warehouses that lined the waterfront near his own restaurant, a black shadow raced from the water side into the road.

Her brake lights flashed.

Adrenaline pumped through Tag's veins.

Had she hit whatever it was…killed it—

Animals touched a soft spot, especially strays. He had a collection of mongrel dogs and cats that lived out back in the woods behind his house.

Her car spun off to the right, bounced over something on the shoulder, and rolled to a crooked stop in front of the alley that ran between two abandoned fish houses. A long shadowy tail disappeared into the tall reedy grasses of the marshy wetlands on the other side of the road.

The junk heap came to a stop right behind her car, ramming her.

The woman in skintight white stumbled out of her sports car.

Rusty and Hank fell on top of her.

Party time.

Tag ripped his bike off road, stopping so fast, he nearly rolled. His right boot hit white shell, and he skidded in a geyser of white dust.

Party time.

Not their party.

His.

He'd been spoiling for a fight…and a woman.

Looks like he had his own personal wish fairy looking out for him up there in heaven.

Frenchy?

Stay with me, Frenchy.

A girl's terrified scream went through Tag like a knife. He was off his bike—running.

Two

Tonight should have been the happiest night of Claire Woods's life. Instead, tears of disillusionment stung her eyes. North had let her drive off. So, now here she was, forty miles from home, her blond hair whipping her face like a mop, and two unsavory goons honking on her tail.

She hit the accelerator. Nothing was turning out the way she'd planned. She had so wanted her wedding to be a fairy tale, but as the big day approached Claire Woods, who everybody thought spoiled and pampered, was feeling bereft and hollow.

If only Melody, her quirky, irrepressible, unpredictable sister, hadn't come home to spoil everything!

It was just like Melody to helicopter off that freighter bound for China and fly home—tonight! Just like her to stage that provocative dance for North's benefit and steal Claire's show and maybe *her* man.

Claire had wanted to shout, "I'm the bride! North loves

me now! Not you!'' But, of course, she'd only stood there with a frozen smile while Melody hummed and did her cute routine.

And North...

''It's not North's fault!''

He hadn't known Melody would pull one of her stunts. Who but Melody would fly in from China just to crash their party? From the second Melody had waltzed into the yacht club ballroom in those tight pants and shimmery blouse, looking like she owned the place, everybody had been electrified. Nobody could stop talking about that buffoon, Merle somebody, a fly-by-night P.I. their daddy had sent to find her six months ago. Melody had laughingly explained how she'd lured Merle on board her China-bound freighter and then tricked him into walking the plank, so to speak.

''Why did you come home?'' North had demanded of Melody. ''Why now?''

''I...I couldn't miss your wedding.''

''You sure missed the last one.'' North's low voice was rapier-sharp.

If North truly loved Claire, he would be chasing Claire right now instead of the two hoods flashing their highbeams and honking behind her.

Instead, her fiancé and her sister were still at the party, probably making eyes at each other this very minute, while she was driving around alone.

No.... No....

A vision of Melody humming softly, Melody, in those skintight black jeans and a white silk shirt, eyes aglow, her honey-gold hair streaming down her slim back took shape in Claire's too-vivid imagination. Her sister's dance had been so enthusiastic, so spontaneous, and so original that everybody had stopped dancing and started clapping the moment she kicked off her shoes and threw them to North. Everyone except North who'd gripped those sparkly high heels in a stranglehold. Not that he hadn't watched her dance, his expression darkening when the other men had started clapping.

How much of her childhood had Claire spent curled up with a book or in her room alone with her dreams while bubbly Melody was out in the yard putting on a show that had all the neighborhood children, especially the boys, spellbound?

Applause and love and sheer sexiness came so easily to the uninhibited Melody.

All her life Claire had wanted to be first with somebody.

"Don't think about Melody," Claire whispered to herself. "Don't think about the pain in North's eyes when he'd watched her dance."

"But I can't stop."

Claire had never outgrown the childish habit of talking to herself, especially when she was in her car alone or primping in front of her mirror.

"Chase me then!" she'd laughingly challenged North a little while after Melody's dance.

The memory made her blush, made her eyes burn. What a brazen fool she was. When would she ever learn North was too cool and mature to play what he called her childish games?

Or was that really it? Did he love her, really love her as once he had loved...

He had told her once, "I can never love you as I loved Melody. But I believe what we'll have will be better and stronger than what I felt for her."

Claire was sick of driving around. More than a little scared, too, and not just of losing North. The jerks behind her were persistent. Her parents' warnings played like tapes in the back of her mind.

A woman alone on the road is prey, Claire. This in a shrill tone from her bossy mother, Dee Dee.

When a man sees a woman alone, he takes it as an invitation. This from Sam, her all-knowing doctor father.

Maybe the old folks were smarter than she'd thought. Her legs had been jelly ever since these two goons had almost sideswiped her, forcing her onto the shoulder a while ago.

The humid wind that battered her face and tangled her butter-colored hair stank with the pungent fragrance of a plankton-laced bay. When their car speeded up, attempting to pass her again, Claire shakily pushed a sticky strand of hair out of her eyes.

Her front wheels skidded. Her heart skittered.

"I'm not scared!"

When the car in her rearview mirror rushed forward and she could no longer see it, she yanked her steering wheel to the left and cut them off. Honking, they eased off the accelerator and veered back into the right lane behind her. So did she. They slowed, and she relaxed enough to rehash the humiliating little scene at the country club with North and Melody, which was the reason she was in this mess.

North never wanted to discuss wedding details, maybe because his first wedding had ended in such disaster.

"We'll all be happier when you grow up!" North had thundered distractedly a few minutes after Melody's dance had ended. Claire had been trying to discuss some of the difficulties with wedding costs. "So, scale back. Compromise!"

North could hold onto his cowboy cool a whole lot longer than most guys, so his uncustomary show of temper should have warned her.

"But I can't. It's our wedding day. If your family would just—"

"You know what your problem is?" North had waved one of Melody's shoes at her. "You're spoiled, Claire."

"Me? Spoiled? You're the big multimillionaire rancher."

Men. At first she hadn't been able to believe that North, whose wealth was legendary, had joined forces with the wedding consultant, caterers, her parents, and his family to attack her. Why couldn't he understand how unsure she felt with Melody home and everybody else pulling her to pieces?

"Darling, Mother keeps saying she just wants our wedding day to be fairy-tale perfect," she'd whispered, "something special we'll remember forever. We're doing this for you…to make up for…" Claire stopped, staring at the sparkly shoes he still held because she couldn't say, *my sister jilting you at the altar.*

"I wish you two would worry a little more about what comes after that day—our marriage."

"Oh, that— That's the happily-ever-after part."

"Damn it." North had shrugged wearily. "I'm beginning to wonder about that."

Finally, she'd said what was really on her mind. "Is this about Melody?"

"Hell, no." But he'd reddened, and the sparkly shoes had glinted. "Life's not lived like the glossy pictures of those bridal and home magazines you and your mother pore over all the time. I wish to hell we'd eloped."

Suddenly she'd realized everyone, especially Melody, had begun watching them when North had raised his voice in annoyance. Claire had felt frightened and guilty when North's gaze had drifted back to her blushing sister.

"I'm sorry," Claire had said. "So sorry. I shouldn't have said anything." When he'd scowled at her and then at the shoes and hadn't apologized, she hadn't known what to do. Suddenly she'd realized she shouldn't have upset him with wedding details right after Melody's dance. "Dance with me, darling,'' she'd pleaded, realizing he hadn't said one word about how beautiful she was in her white sheath.

Again his black gaze had drifted to Melody. ''I'm really not in the mood to put on a show!''

''But we're supposed to be madly in love.''

''Claire, your sister's show is a hard act to follow. And now you've got me all worked up, too. I can't just... You're always pressuring me, chasing me—''

''''Cause you never chase me.''

His black eyes left Melody and flicked over Claire with a strange look of pity that startled them both. When he pressed his handsome lips together and continued to regard her thoughtfully, she was terrified.

''How will it look to everybody if we just stand around, not dancing, not talking?'' Claire pleaded. ''And holding my sister's shoes?''

''Frankly, I don't much give a damn.''

''You'd better be careful,'' Melody had quipped, gliding up to them. ''That sounds a lot like Rhett Butler's exit line.''

A look had passed between Melody and North. Then North's face had hardened and he slammed the shoes into her open palms. ''And you're just the girl to appreciate a good exit line.''

Melody had gone as pale as death.

Claire had felt a burst of sympathy for North.

Would he ever get over her sister?

Of course, he would. He was. She had just been immature to push him.

Would he ever be over her sister?

People were turning to stare. Not knowing what to do, Claire had flown out of the club and gone to her car.

North would follow. He would leave the stuffy party where all anybody ever did was try to impress each other. He would chase her. He had to.

Nobody had been more upset than Dee Dee when Claire's wacky, unconventional sister had broken North's heart. Just as nobody had been more elated when he'd found consolation first in Claire's friendship, and then in her love.

Claire banged her hands on her steering wheel and listened to the band. Even out here the throbbing music was loud, almost loud enough to drown out the loneliness in her young aching heart, almost.

"Go back inside."

"No, any minute North will march out those polished mahogany doors with the shiny brass handles and prove his love for me—to everyone."

But the doors didn't open, and the brass handles began to swim in a sea of hot tears. North stayed at the club.

And even though Claire had known deep down that she was, at least, partly in the wrong—she hadn't had the guts to go back inside, face Melody and meekly apologize to North.

Her mother, Dee Dee, who'd all but engineered this marriage after Melody had jilted North, was, once again, planning the wedding of the year. Only Dee Dee was determined that Claire's wedding would be so magnificent everybody would forget and forgive what Melody had done. But the financial burden of marrying great wealth for the second time was a strain on their upper-middle-class budget, a fact her father never let Dee Dee forget, which was why Claire had asked North to help.

"Have a wedding your family can afford," he'd said. "After what Melody pulled, all that matters is a sacred ceremony."

Mother said the wedding had to be perfect...perfect. Just the event to reestablish Dee Dee Woods as a Texas hostess to be reckoned with after having been made the laughing-stock of the town last year by Melody. The effort and pressure to impress the right people had her mother in bed with what she called ''heat'' headaches.

Bridal nerves. Maybe that's what had Claire so uptight and jittery lately…even before Melody's return.

The moon lit a path from the horizon to the shoreline. Not that she noticed when the jerks behind her honked loudly.

Their bumper slammed into hers. A sickening chill of fear shivered up her spine.

She had driven forty miles on this fool's errand to regain her pride. Halfway to Rockport where her parents had a condo on the bay, the punks had forced her onto the shoulder.

They honked flirtily again. Somehow she had to get back to North and apologize, really apologize. But first she had to shake these juvenile delinquents before she left Rockport.

When the hoods flashed their high beams, she stomped down on the accelerator of her sports car.

It was now or never.

As the cars raced, she began to practice her apology.

''Oh, North, I'm sorry. You were right and I was wrong. You're my best friend.'' She would close her long lashes, let them drift open slowly. ''Of course, I love you just as I know you love me. Seeing Melody… Those shoes… That dance… I just wanted you to chase me… To excite me… To thrill me… To act like a caveman for once.''

The way Loverboy does.

''You can't say that to North Black!'' an irreverent masculine voice in her head drawled.

''I know that, silly.'' She couldn't ever let North…or anyone else know about her embarrassing, secret, fantasy life with…with Loverboy.

The trouble had started innocently, the way most bad things do. A lonely little girl, Claire hadn't ever been able to make friends as easily as Melody. And if she had made a friend, Melody had quickly charmed her or him.

Claire had worn lace dresses when Melody and the other girls wore jeans. Claire had read books, while Melody and her friends had made mud pies and climbed trees. Finally, Claire had invented an imaginary friend, Hal, who was just as lonely and shy as she was. Everybody had thought it was so cute the way she included him in every conversation, set a special place for him, even bought presents for him. Somehow over the years, Hal had grown up and gotten way too sexy for her to handle. She was a virgin...but only technically. In her imagination, Hal and she got up to wanton mischief in all sorts of dark and inappropriate locations, on kitchen tables and the hood of her car. Hal was tall with black hair...like North.

And yet not like North at all.

North didn't have all that much time for her. He kept much of himself hidden from her. He was steady and predictable when it came to his work, too tied to the responsibilities of his ranching empire and his duties to his legendary family.

Hal was wild and dangerous and free, insidiously attentive, and as faceless as an outlaw's shadow.

North could give her the kind of safe, secure life her upper-middle-class mother could brag about.

Mostly her imaginary lover was a pirate on a ship who carried her off to sea. Sometimes he was a bandit or a highwayman who carried her to his hideout and robbed her of more than her gold.

Strip, my lady. Slowly. And every time she took something off, he would toss a gold coin at her feet.

Mostly she dreamed about him at night, but lately she'd been having the most lurid daydreams. The oversexed phantom was becoming terribly distracting. One reason she was so anxious to get married was to send Loverboy packing. Once North made love to her, she would have a husband to dream about. What sane woman would chase a dream, when she had a man like North in her bed? Everybody, simply everybody told her North was the sexiest, hottest, richest cowboy prince in all of Texas.

North could have chosen any woman. He had chosen her.

"That's not the way it was, *Sugar-Baby,*" purred Loverboy.

She hated to be called that. "Shut up, Hal!"

"I was there! *And Melody was first!*"

"Go away and leave me alone!"

"Never. I am not abandoning you till I find a more suitable companion for you."

"Stay out of my love life!"

Suddenly a strange thing happened. The black sky turned pink, and she saw a lone black figure on a motorcycle off to her left silhouetted in a white cone of light. Pinkish-blue light pulsated around him. He was wearing a helmet, but the heat of his gaze was a visceral, physical connection. Even in that blurred, peripheral glimpse, she sensed that such a man in the flesh might prove wilder and more chaotically thrilling than any secret interior existence with Loverboy.

She knew better than to look at the biker, but some dark and dangerous force compelled her.

Curiosity kills more than cats.

The forbidden—especially in the tame, pampered life of a woman like Claire, who lived her life by rules the way some people paint by numbers—was the most powerful temptation. Besides, Melody's dance and North's dark mood had opened a crack in her heart and self-esteem.

She was on the brink of marriage to the most desirable of men. Never had she felt less sexually attractive, nor more afraid or vulnerable. What was the biker doing alone in a dark cemetery?

Jauntily, she turned toward him. For the space of a heart-beat her long-lashed eyes fixed on the black helmet that hid his face with an avidity that should have shamed her. Then with a will all its own, her glossily tipped fingernail tooted her horn.

He nodded. Her lips parted coquettishly. But when the biker skidded out onto the road after her, her heart jumped into her throat.

The thunder of his big bike racing to catch up to her was a fuse that lit a primal heat in every nerve in her body.

The biker left asphalt, caught up with her pursuers, spewing gravel on them before braking and then falling in behind them.

She knew he was bad.

Bad to the bone.

Why did she suddenly feel she was on a collision course with destiny? She turned her three-carat engagement ring backwards.

North was in Corpus, but the chase was on.

Three

―――

"**Y**ou're driving too fast!" Claire's voice sounded panicky as she raced past the entrance to her parents' condo. Not that she had any intention of leading the pack straight to her door.

She didn't know what to do, how to get away from the hoods or the biker. Why weren't there any other cars on the road? Fulton was deserted, the restaurants shut down, the warehouses locked up.

Suddenly a black cat dashed out from under a pile of construction rubbish right in front of her.

"Oh, my God!"

She honked, slammed on the brakes, swerving off the pavement, careening toward two shadowy buildings surrounded by scaffolding.

"Stupid!"

Then she bounced over a pile of discarded roof shingles. Her front left tire blew on a nail and she bumped to a stop.

The jerks rolled right up behind her and nudged her back bumper.

"Oh, no!"

They gunned their engine, then killed it.

She was caught in the dark tunnel between two buildings with a fence at one end and them behind her. Scaffolding cast eerie bars of light and shadow.

"Oh, dear." Claire's shaking hands fumbled in her over-stuffed purse. A package of tissues, her change purse, and her keys fell out.

Behind her, car doors banged open. Glowing cigarette butts were pitched onto the shell drive and ground into pulp beneath bootheels. Like a pair of raptors, they eyed her edgily, their hostile faces framed for a second or two in her rearview mirror.

One glance had her heart beating like a jungle drum, her fingers shaking so hard their tips went numb.

Where was it?

Headlights rushed by.

"Help me! Somebody help me!"

The sedan's red taillights vanished into the dark.

Her trembling fingertips closed over her cell phone. Peering over her door, she got a glimpse of a dirty T-shirt and black tank top, slashed jeans before she began backing down the alley.

"Well, looky, looky, Rusty." The dark, skinny guy with the mean, narrow face lit a cigarette, took a drag.

Rusty, a greasy blonde built like a tank, snatched the cigarette, inhaling deeply.

Gripping her phone, she got out of her car, stumbling down the dark alley between the two white-washed buildings. Rusty followed, laughing, his heavy heels crunching shell, his long shadow curling around her like a black snake.

No! No!

Before she could punch in in the numbers 9-1-1, they had her cornered against a springy, cyclone fence topped with razorwire. She clawed. Chain-link chimed.

The greasy blonde's thick fist snatched the phone and threw it on the ground. His face loomed. His blue irises blazed scarily brighter. "We wuz looking for somebody."

Throaty male laughter.

"Looks like you're our consolation prize."

She broke into an icy sweat. She made little low sounds deep in her throat.

The large freckled hand reached for her diamond necklace. Paralyzed, she endured his touch. He stroked her lip, brushed her cheek, his dirty fingers obscenely gentle, his leering smile horrible. She squeezed her eyes shut as that unbearable hand explored, but she couldn't stop the tears that slowly beaded her long black lashes and leaked silently down her cheeks.

Rusty's hand traced the shape of her mouth.

She opened her eyes. With a deceptive smile, she bravely met his feral blue stare. His tongue lolled as he unzipped his jeans and moved in for the kill. Quick as a turtle, she bit his filthy, thick finger.

On a yelp of pain, he jumped back.

She screamed and ran.

The skinny one jumped her and knocked her to the ground. Her head struck a brick. Stars spun in a white sky above the palm trees. They fell on top of her, grabbed her wrists, pinning her body with knees that dug hard into her belly. The last thing she saw was those overbright white eyes. The last thing she felt was the pain in her head, in her neck, in her shoulders. The last thing she heard was their voices, telling her how much she wanted them.

Dimly she heard her silk sheath ripping, then their belt buckles unsnapping, leather sliding through denim loops. But when they knelt over her again, there was a monstrou roar from the other end of the alley. Fantails of white shell and powdery dust spewed above her.

"Rusty! Hank! She's mine!" thundered a deep male voice from the end of the alley.

Loverboy? she wondered woozily.

"Holy damn! It's him!"

"Frenchy's murderer!" Hank spat. A switchblade snapped, flashing silver.

"Get, before I send you to hell along with Frenchy!" A black barrel flashed. She saw a dark hand. Then the black hole at the end of an automatic. "Get—out of my town—permanently."

She saw flame, heard a pop.

"You heard me. Get off her. She's mine."

Pop. Pop. Pop. Loose shells pinged when the bullets hit dirt. Miraculously, she wasn't hurt. The cruel hands on her body loosened.

She opened her eyes and saw two figures furtively scuffling past her on bloody hands and knees, their lank hair falling forward. Car doors slammed as the other man's shadow fell over her.

"This ain't a free peep show. Get!"

The pair cursed, started their engine, and roared away, leaving her alone—with *him.*

Maybe she should've felt afraid. But she was too numb.

All was silent save for the palm trees rustling above her. She swallowed. Vaguely she tasted shell dust and that awful tobacco-stained finger.

Shell crunched under a man's heavy boots. Then his low, hard voice cracked. "You gonna get up? Or are you really out for a good time?"

Her eyes snapped open and shot fire.

Wide-spread black boots were planted mere inches from her face. Her gaze climbed a virile, masculine body packed into denim so tight the cloth looked painted on.

He had a lean waist, a shapely torso, and a linebacker's squared-off, wide shoulders. A bright halo backlighted a well-shaped ebony head. His untamed hair was longish, and like a pirate, he sported a silver earring. They must've hurt him because he was pressing a white handkerchief against his cheek, sopping blood.

She couldn't see the fierce face that went with this diabolical individual, but his bold, stripping gaze made her shiver.

Was this over-sexed caveman with the massive biceps a figment of her maddeningly-fertile imagination? She shut her eyes, willing him to disappear. When she opened them, the scuffed black boots were an inch closer.

The biker jammed the black automatic into his waistband, his bloody handkerchief into his pocket and kneeled down.

"They...they called you a murderer."

"You gonna believe scum...or the man who just saved you?"

She didn't know how to answer this beast.

"Do you know how to say thank you, pretty lady?"

His hard gaze knocked the breath out of her.

"Because you owe me—big time," he murmured, "and I can think of any number of ways for a woman like you to thank a man like me. The night is young—"

A woman like you? "You have some nerve."

"So do you...running around at this hour...in that car. In that body. Where were you going? What were you looking for?" He laughed derisively. "I know your type."

"I don't want to know yours!"

His blazing eyes settled on her face, moved lower with an overabundance of feral sensuality. "You wanna bet?"

"Just go!"

"You're too weak to get up, too rude to say thank you, too much of a liar to admit what you are.... You have a flat tire which you probably don't know how to change. You're half-naked and lying flat on your good-looking tush in a most seductive pose—'' There was no mistaking the sexually-charged innuendo in his low tone. "I don't blame you for wanting something wild. I was on the prowl for the same thing myself.''

"Half-naked?'' Her brain stalled. Alarm bells jangled. "What—?''

She shut up when the biker wrapped his arms around her in the darkness. When he touched her, she got the sexual charge she'd been waiting for her whole life.

From him.

She was too shocked to resist as he began to check for bruises and other injuries. His fingers on her skin just got hotter and hotter.

Instantaneous man-woman combustion.

Waves of erotic heat lapped her like a turbulent wake.

He tensed.

She froze.

"See! I was right about you," he said.

"Take your hands off me!''

He laughed and then jerked her unceremoniously from the ground. Strands of her torn white silk skirt tickled her bare thighs as he pulled her to her feet. When she collapsed against him, his large, sure hands caught her.

More dizzying heat.

Blood from the cut on his cheek smeared the right half of his face. There was a dark stain on his white T-shirt, too. He had gotten hurt because of her. Her expression softened as she studied his rich black hair, his mouth, and then the cut.

"It's a scratch," he muttered.

"Maybe you should put something on it.''

His eyes went dark with dislike. "Don't act like you give a damn.''

"Are you always this rude? Or are you just showing off for me?"

His brows slanted. He studied her and then suddenly he laughed again.

She smiled. That broke the ice a bit. Then the air between them began to thicken again a little like sauce left to simmer over a fire. He was gorgeous, if a girl went for all male...and lethal. Which she certainly didn't.

Nonetheless, she couldn't stop looking at him. And that made her blush.

"Who are you?" she whispered, trying to push him away even though some part of her wanted to be locked in those warm muscular arms forever.

"You don't care who I am."

"Were you friends...with them?"

"No." He didn't explain.

"I hit my head when I fell," she said. "I'm a little woozy. Not...not myself. This feels like a bad dream."

His hands combed tangled, golden hair and found the blood-crusted bump on the back of her head.

She jerked away. "Ouch!"

"You have a lump the size of a hen's egg there. You need a doctor—"

"No doctor!"

Black eyebrows arched. "You're in no position to give me orders, princess."

"Nobody can know about this."

"About me, you mean." His gaze slid over her hips, down her legs.

Her legs! She experienced a full-body blush. Their entire length was exposed to his view. Her silk skirt was shredded. Strips of the gauzy stuff were curling high above her thighs. Why, he could probably see her panties!

Panties!

Melody and her little jokes!

Claire wasn't wearing pant—

Frantic fingers tugged modestly at the remnants of white silk to cover panties that simply didn't exist.

"Don't bother." His eyes had narrowed, the intimacy in his gaze and raw whisper shaming her. "Black lace. Thong. And your voluptuous body to pull it off."

She recoiled, her blush reheating.

"Very becoming," he said.

Melody had given her the thong panties as a joke tonight. When she'd tried them on in the ladies' room, Melody had dared her to wear them.

"Thong-bikini," he jeered softly. "A deliberate turn-on."

"For a man like you maybe."

"Careful! You're the one in the naughty underwear—Like I said—you were asking for it."

"Your jeans are two sizes too tight!"

His handsome mouth quirked. "A nice girl wouldn't notice."

That was the sort of teasing boast Loverboy was always making…when she got undressed…when she was scrubbing herself between her legs in intimate places with a washcloth beneath foaming bubbles in her bathtub.

"Shut up, Loverboy!"

His avid grin was white against his sun-darkened skin. "What did you call me?"

"Nothing!"

He dazzled her with another smile. "You talk to yourself then?"

"Mind your own business!" Her drop-dead glare made that smile of his broaden, gentling those rugged features; she found his smile so charming it almost undid her fierce resolve to dislike him.

If his jeans were tight, his white shirt was equally tight, revealing way too much muscle and black furred chest.

"You shouldn't strip a guy with those big baby blues...'cause he might take you up on that invitation."

She couldn't quit looking at him. The light seemed better, or she was more accustomed to the gloom. His tense, carved features held a powerful fascination for her. Suddenly she was studying the tiny white scar above his brow, the nose that had been broken. With a moan, she reached up and feathered a fingertip across the jagged white mark above his arcing brow.

Velvet fingertip against his warm, tanned forehead. Her unexpected touch and the inexplicable tenderness in her gaze brought wary turbulence to his silver eyes.

A shadow swept his face, and she saw naked vulnerability. He wrenched her hand away so fast she cried out. With a wordless scowl, he strode toward her car.

"What did I do?" she cried, running to catch up to him.

He whirled. "You don't give a damn about me any more than I give a damn about you!"

"So...you're scared, too."

His panicky eyes grew colder.

She was sure she'd seen his softer side. Ignoring his sudden tension, she smilingly moved toward him. The urge to cup his chin in her soft fingers sent a chill through her.

"Women like you want only one thing," he said.

"Really?" This time she laughed.

"Open your trunk," he growled. "Show me your spare."

When she didn't budge, he strode past her, back down the alley. In the darkness he leaned down and picked up her cell phone. When he brought it back and handed it to her, his fingers accidentally grazed hers. He tore his hand away, but not in time. Jolted by the same charge, the phone slid through her fingers.

"Hey..." With lightning-fast reflexes he caught it and jammed it into her open palm, closing each of her fingers, one at a time, around the black plastic. He wasn't exactly caressing her, but her knees felt shaky.

The savage downward flick of his dark brow, told her she disturbed him, too. His glinting eyes swept her from head to toe, lingering on her breasts where she clasped her phone.

"Is every damn thing you do deliberately sexy?" he rasped.

"What?" Parting her lips, she leaned forward.

"Did you tease those guys for the hell of it too?" He caught her to him. "You rich girls are all alike. You make us dream, lust, and you don't even see us...except when you want *this*."

She struggled, but he didn't let her go.

That got her mad and scared. But it was too late for both of them.

He didn't want to kiss her.

She didn't want to be kissed.

But faster than either of them could blink or think, his hard mouth was on hers, and her lips opened as his tongue met hers with a needy desire that under ordinary circumstances would have humiliated her.

"You can't get this in your safe little world. That's why you came looking for it tonight. Well, baby, you're gonna get what you were looking for after all."

In the next instant, he slammed her against the wall of the warehouse, and she loved it. His eyes flamed. His dark, carved face lowered to hers again.

She should have fought.

Melting into him, she surrendered to his devouring kisses. One hard hand yanked her zipper down, moved under her white silk bodice, inside it, his long fingers shaping and caressing her satin throat, her breasts, stroking her pink, pearly nipples till they peaked. Then she felt his warm tongue there, laving those tender tips as she arched against his mouth.

He knew how to touch, where to touch to set her on fire. When she wiggled closer, his other hand tore her thong bikini down and slid his hand into the wetness there.

"This is wrong," she managed in a hoarse whisper.

"You started it," he taunted.

With a groan, he cupped her bottom, pulled her legs up, wrapping them around his hips, holding her up easily. Her heart rushed, slowed, rushed again. Never ever had she done anything like this before. But then this wasn't real. This had to be fantasy.

Her fingertips explored his sandpaper rough jaw, combed through his coarse black hair. His mouth and hands and body were so hot, so hard...and yet so infinitely gentle. Never, ever had she felt so flamingly, completely, sensually alive. So close to such a vitally explosive edge. Her whole world was a molten whirlpool with him at the center.

She yanked his leather jacket down over his shoulders, smothering kisses against his throat, tasting his skin, even the caked blood there, all the while murmuring, "Yes...yes...."

A car roared by, the white glare of headlights exposing them.

His kiss stopped instantly.

"Do you want it like this? In a back alley? With a man whose name you don't even know? I'm game if you are."

He was real. This was real.

Outraged, she stared at him. He was low-class and barbaric. What was *her* excuse? One kiss and she'd sunk to his level.

Shock made her cheeks flame. Shame made her shiver. What had gotten into her?

Shaking, she collapsed against the rough wooden wall.

Abruptly his hands on her hips fell away, and he lowered her body to the ground.

"Now that was a thank-you," he whispered hoarsely.

She fell back against the unpainted boards. As she rubbed her eyes, her pulse thudded violently. Her skin was drenched with perspiration.

Five-hundred wedding invitations had been mailed. Wedding gifts were stacked to the ceiling in her mother's den. North, who'd already been jilted once, would be devastated if she publicly humiliated him a second time. And her mother...

After Melody had vanished, the constantly-busy, gregarious Dee Dee had sat in a dark corner of her living room for days, not bothering to put on her makeup, lunch with her friends, or run her house.

The wedding was three weeks away. Claire had made irrevocable choices. Her mother had invested months in this project.

Her rescuer—if that was what he was—was furious. His silver eyes blazed with lethally fierce emotion.

He is so beautiful, she thought.

"Let's get your trunk open," he whispered. When she didn't move: "Move!" he roared.

"Okay... okay...." Quickly she scampered toward her car, clumsily yanking at the clump of keys dangling from her ignition. Instead of handing the keys to him, self-consciously she lifted her hand above his, dropping them into his open palm, careful not to touch so much as a callused fingertip.

Suddenly their not touching was almost worse than touching. His silver eyes studied her too knowingly, reminding her that a moment ago she'd melted against him. Body and soul, she'd been his for the taking.

When she began to shake, he tore off his leather jacket.

"Cover yourself! I'm a beast," he murmured viciously, "driven mad by lust for you. Trash."

Her thoughts to a *T*. She reddened, felt shamed.

Again she had to ask herself—what was she?

Her fingers closed around soft leather. "Thanks," she whispered. When she slid into the garment that held his heat and male scent, her womb contracted so violently, she almost ripped the jacket off.

Quickly he had her trunk open and her jack and tire thrown out on the ground. He worked fast, furiously loosening the lug nuts, jacking the car. She stood over him, trying not to think of the kiss, admiring his skill with the heavy work. Focusing on him made her wonder who he was and what had happened to him.

"You must have been very handsome before…"

When he tilted his black head at her, his hard gaze sent an embarrassed trill of sensation through her lower belly.

She gasped self-consciously. "Before…before the accident," she continued.

"What accident?" The bleakness in his dark tone scared her.

After that he worked in silence. Ten minutes later he was done.

He slammed her trunk shut, dusted his broad, brown palms together, and ensnared her in another hot glance.

"Thanks," she whispered, heat spreading through her. She started to shrug out of his jacket, but he stopped her.

"Keep it. Get in." Like a well-bred gentleman, he opened her door. "I'll follow you home."

Manners. *Where had he learned manners?*

"No."

"Where do you live?"

"I'd rather not say."

"You're not driving home alone till we get your tire fixed then."

"I'll be fine."

"You rich girls too spoiled to compromise, princess?"

She resented his sharp tone. "As if you've known so many."

"Too many."

"I—I...I'm not spoiled!"

"Prove it." He tossed her her keys and slung a long leg over his bike.

"But—"

"I know a mechanic who works late."

She sank back against her leather seat. "But—"

"His shop. Or I follow you home. Right to your doorstep. It's your choice, princess."

"Don't call me princess!"

At the garage, the biker did not relinquish command. At first his retro behavior made her feel awkward. Then it really got under her skin.

It was *her* tire; *her* car.

When she had taken all the domination and arrogance she could take, she went up to him and thumped him on his wide shoulder. "You can go."

He cocked a dark brow.

"I'm an adult," she said.

"You're also a woman. A woman who's gotten into more than her share of trouble for one night."

"You have no right to tell me what to do."

"Well, you're not getting into any more— Not on my shift—*princess.*"

The mechanic, a skinny guy with a skimpy goatee, smiled at the conclusion of this humiliating exchange. To make matters worse, he kept peeping at her from underneath her car, his eyes almost popping out of his head every time he got a glimpse of her legs.

The biker circled her car, barking orders. He insisted that all the fluid levels be checked as well as the air pressure in all her tires. When her car was nearly done, he joined her on the shabby automobile backseat where she sat in a shadowy corner of the garage.

"Since we're all done, you really can go," she whispered. "I can pay him and—"

"I'm not leaving you here alone…in the middle of the night."

"I can take care of myself." Her voice sounded surer than she felt.

His rugged face was implacable. "The way you did in the alley?"

Her gaze fell. She didn't want to remember her feelings of utter helplessness when those thugs had knocked her to the ground.

She began to shake, her eyes to glisten.

"Anybody would've been scared," he said.

"I—I don't want you to see me…like this, but I don't want you to go, either. I want— I want—" Suddenly she was too overwhelmed by her emotions to go on.

When he bent closer, her hands reached out for him, blindly clutching at his sleeves, then tugging him closer, gripping his muscled arms. When he lifted her and pulled her against him, settling her closer, her hands wound around his neck, and she clung, holding onto him with a fierce incomprehensible need, her breath slicing in short gasps.

"I thought they…" She broke off shudderingly.

His fingers brushed her cheek. "*They* didn't."

"I—I hate the way you think I'm an idiot."

His arms pressed her against the long, hard length of him, and he began to rock back and forth, his compassion so genuine she was moved. "Don't. Hush."

"All done," rang a tinny, too curious voice behind them.

When the biker tried to ease her out of his arms, she was

too shaken in some deep fathomless way to let him go. She began to cry and to tremble all over.

"Why don't we get some coffee somewhere? You're in no condition to drive," he said. "I could call someone—"

"No! Nobody must know…about this!"

"About me, you mean." His silver eyes hardened. But his voice softened. "Why don't we go to my place…just till you feel better?"

Only after he uttered this absurdity, did she relax and let him go. Dimly she was aware of him paying, of him negotiating with the mechanic to leave his bike there for the night.

"Come on," he whispered.

Her tears had drained her. Her legs felt like leaden weights.

He took her hands in his. "Sweetheart, he's closing."

Vaguely, she watched his lips move. She tried to concentrate, but his words ran together like jibberish.

Instead of obeying him, she reached up to touch the bloody place on his face.

"We have to get you home," he said.

Home. As if it were a place they shared.

Almost, almost she wished it was.

She remembered the alley, the shells tearing her silk sheath, the brutal hands on her bare skin.

Her head throbbed. Then a belated wave of dizzying blackness crashed over her.

"Oh, baby," she heard him say right before he caught her.

When she woke up, it was as if she were in a dream. Her clothes were gone. Somebody had bathed all the white dust and blood from her scratched skin. She was in a rustic house that smelled of wet grasses and the sea as well as the nearby marshes. She lay between sheets scented with laundry soap. She heard crickets and cicadas and night frogs. Unlike most houses in Texas, his was on the water, and not air-conditioned. The windows were screened to let in cool, salt-scented breezes. Banana leaves rustled against the screens and beyond she could hear the lap of waves. The natural smells and humid air brought back her childhood when she'd spent more time outside running free in backyards...on wet sandy beaches.

Then *his* black head stirred on her pillow and she made out his harsh features in the shimmering moonlight.

She was in *his* bed. Underneath *his* cotton sheet, snuggled companionably against his long, male body.

When she opened her mouth to scream, his predatory silver eyes burned into hers. Then a big hand clamped down on her lips.

When she fought to twist away, he held her frightened glance wordlessly.

"No, no," she whispered, pushing at him.

He rolled on top of her, his big body pinning her to the soft mattress. "I won't hurt you."

He stroked her cheek until she stilled. When she closed her eyes, he loosened his hold. But she remained in his arms and reveled in his velvet touch as she listened to the night sounds.

His fingertips burned her up, tracing the shape of her eyelashes and brows, caressing her lips and the curve of her nose. His exquisite gentleness made her quiver.

But his gentleness mixed with her own physical needs was not what drew her into the vortex. It was more, much more. Some part of her remembered him carrying her inside, holding her close, comforting her.

His touch was so soothing, his eyes intense. He made her feel so special, so cared for, so loved—*his*. Which was odd. She had North, who was her dear friend...her family. But this man was touched by her vulnerability as they weren't.

Why hadn't she ever felt like this before? So complete? Like she mattered for herself? She'd always had to jump through hoops for love. She'd had to make good grades. She'd had to be beautiful, dutiful. Perfect. She'd had to prove that she was better than the son her father had wanted. Had to prove herself to North's family. She'd had to follow her bossy mother's orders. And always Melody had been there. Melody, with her sunny disposition and impish sense of humor. Melody, the show-off, who was so effortlessly, so easily loved.

With this man Claire could be herself. She could simply be.

Your daddy cried when the nurse told him you were a girl.

All her life Claire had had to prove to her father that she was even better than precious Harry who had died. Harry who would have been perfect if he had lived.

But no matter what she'd done, she'd never measured up to her family's expectations or to her own.

When the biker withdrew his hand from her face, she felt infinitely calmed. She took his long, lean fingers in hers, manipulating them, kissing them one by one, thanking him for his unique gift which was acceptance.

When she was done, his gray eyes stared straight into hers.

"How can this be?" she whispered. "How can we be?"

"You came looking for this."

"No."

"Admit it."

Their gazes clashed. Then a powerful gust slapped the banana leaves against the house. A shutter came loose and began to bang. He got up, padded out of the room on bare feet, then down the breezeway to secure it. When he came back, he lay beside her once again.

She was too afraid to move, to speak. Too afraid of her intense, inexplicable needs.

Afraid of his, too.

And yet she was more afraid of the loneliness in her real life, of the loneliness she would return to when this dream with him had spun its course.

She closed her eyes and pretended she was asleep. He let her pretend, and soon, all too soon, she really was.

Her childhood nightmare came back to her.

She was lost. All alone in the dark. Cut off from her family and love.

Terrified.

Four

Claire was lost and running. It was so dark she couldn't see. Then someone called her name.

"Sugar-Baby."

She shot bolt upright to moonlight flowing in a slant across an immense bed. A ceiling fan crouched, undulating above her like a giant black spider. She shuddered, trying to make sense of weird groupings of shadows and shapes in the unfamiliar room. A monstrous ladderback chair draped with a man's black leather jacket stood out like a frieze against the white wooden wall.

"It was just a bad dream," rumbled a deep, sleepy voice beside her. "No more bad guys. You're safe in bed...with me—*Sugar-Baby*."

Sugar-Baby. Loverboy's pet nickname.

His silver earring glinted wickedly from the dark.

The biker!

"You kept saying Sugar-Baby and Loverboy in your sleep."

Slowly the incredible man beside her came into focus. She saw amused, gray eyes and heavy, black brows. A crop of untidy, blue-black hair toppled over his wide forehead. His features, even his long nose that had been broken, his stubborn chin, all seemed carved of some polished, dark wood. His shoulders were dangerously broad. If he wasn't exactly handsome, he was smolderingly masculine. Strangely, she wasn't scared of him at all.

Yawning lazily, he rolled away from her, carrying the sheet off her.

Naked, she hugged her breasts and then yanked the sheet back.

He laughed, unashamed that she'd stripped him of all but his tough, brown hide. "You were sweeter asleep."

She shot him a dirty look only to gasp when she saw how much of his rampant male form was sprawled beside her.

Hastily she lowered her gaze, but not before the impression of his muscular frame and black-furred chest had burned an indelible image into her brain.

"Where are your clothes?"

"You swiped the sheet, my lady!"

"Oh…" Quickly she tugged the bottom end loose from the massive bed frame and threw it at his middle.

"Thanks." He covered the essentials and lay back, pillowing his head in the crook of his dark arms.

His stare brought a self-conscious blush. Or was it the awareness of his well-shaped, dusky body lying right next to her under the sheet that had her so rattled?

Primly she bunched her end of the sheet at her throat. "I've got to go."

"Not till the sun comes up, pretty lady."

"Who made you my jailer?"

"Your keeper, my pet. Think of me as your knight in

shining armor…er…who risked his life fighting to save your honor.''

"I don't see any armor."

"It's uncomfortable in bed."

"And as for saving my honor— You didn't have the slightest intention—"

"I thought you were looking for a man who turned you on. Forgive me for offering my services."

His coarse whisper and quick, irreverent grin caught her off guard. Tangible need raced like quicksilver through her veins. But when a brown arm reached for her, she scooted to the edge of the bed. Scooping up the chenile spread, she wrapped herself up like an outraged mummy.

"Where's your bathroom?"

"Sugar-Baby, I prefer to snuggle when I first wake up."

"Don't call me that! Where—"

Grinning, he nodded toward a door, and she bolted.

Whiskers leaned into the brush, bit at it, slapped at it and then hurled himself onto the kitchen throw rug, enthusiastically rolling, purring as Tag stroked his fat black tummy.

"You're hooked on this, aren't you, old fella?"

Whiskers slapped the brush out of his hand and arrogantly padded over to his empty bowl.

The first time Tag saw Whiskers, he'd been a puny, half-starved kitten eating garbage in a culvert pipe.

"Had enough, old fella?"

Tag pitched the brush under the sink. He'd been grooming the cat while he waited on her.

Hell.

Sipping from a mug of coffee, Tag strode from the kitchen to the bathroom door for the third time since she'd locked herself inside.

She'd cracked the door, and he could see inside. She was

looking at herself, making dramatic faces, whispering to the mirror.

A big diamond flashed when she waved her left hand. She must've seen it when he did because she gasped. Quickly she removed the ring and stuffed it into a small bag that she put in her purse.

A few minutes later she tiptoed out.

"What took you so long?" he demanded.

At the sound of his voice, she froze.

"You look good in my clothes, pretty lady. Sexy!"

Startled, she ran her hand down his shirt. Her fingers smoothed the soft, black cotton over her lush breasts so that her nipples peaked. She was engaged to another man. Yet she'd showered in his bathroom and was standing in his bedroom looking flushed and fresh and too alluring to believe.

"They're way too big," she said.

"Yes." The baggy, black shirt and jeans left a lot to his imagination. But since he already knew what a terrific body she had, keeping it hidden tantalized him. And that hair— Tangled as it was in that awful ponytail that made her look like a smart-ass thirteen-year-old, those golden tresses were the rarest shade of yellow silk. He'd touched them, wrapped his fingers round and round in the soft masses when she'd trustingly laid her head on his chest in her sleep. Her eyes were a dark and luminous blue-blue. And yet innocent. So charmingly, sweetly innocent.

When she slept, she hadn't been afraid of him.

"Black is definitely your color," he muttered.

Against that dark hue, her skin seemed paler and yet incandescent in the moonlight. Even without makeup, her kissable lips were ruby-red. To look at her was a sensual feast.

It felt good having her in his house. She fit. Belonged.
The ring.

She was engaged. Like the rich women who came to Shorty's, she had a safe, rich man on the string.

He wanted to grab her now, to have it done with, to lose himself in her flesh, get her out of his system, to prove she was like all the others. Yet he didn't want to spoil it.

"I watched you through the crack…primping…."

"How dare—"

"When you put on my shirt, you spun round and round…like a little girl playing dress-up."

She tossed her ponytail and pointed her nose in the air.

His eyes fell to her lips and then to her breasts. "Only not like a little girl at all."

Her flush deepened.

"Who were you talking to in there?"

She swallowed. "Nobody."

He smiled. "You have quite an imagination."

"Mother says it's a failing."

"Do you want a cup of coffee?"

When she nodded, smiling at this safer topic of conversation, he led her to the kitchen.

As he poured the strong, black, steaming gourmet brew, he couldn't stop staring at the creamy curve of her neck which was revealed because she hadn't buttoned the top two buttons of his shirt. He wondered if she'd left them that way just to tempt him. Whatever. Her skin glowed like honey against his black shirt.

It was a crazy, dangerous feeling, but for an instant he felt like he was back in New Orleans when his father had first adopted him. He felt like he could be happy with this woman, that he would do anything to win her respect and admiration.

"Are you hungry?" he whispered roughly, resenting the way she stirred long-abandoned hopes and dreams.

She nodded too vigorously. He suspected that she just

wanted to keep him busy at something she deemed harmless.

"How about an omelette?"

"Anything."

Her breathy answer hung in his imagination as he put his heavy frying pan on a gas burner, lit the jet, cracked eggs into the pan with a splatter. *Anything.* In no time he was beside her at the table sharing a fluffy omelette and toast.

"You're a good cook," she said.

"A sensitive cook. I like my guests to eat every bite and brag on me."

She smiled impishly. "This is the best omelette I've ever eaten in my whole life."

He hated himself for basking in her praise, for waiting for more.

"Every single bite is pure rapture."

"Ah, rapture." Another word to hang there in his imagination. He'd show her rapture. He wanted to lick her golden hairline. To slide his hand beneath black cotton and cup her breasts. To rip those jeans she was wearing off. To brand her as his.

"Rapture. I like the sound of that. Keep talking, pretty lady."

She laughed between bites. "You could be a chef...." She shot him a megawatt smile.

I'd rather be your lover. He grinned sheepishly, ashamed of the egotistical pleasure he found in her compliments. "Okay. Okay."

"And you're a good host."

That surprised him. He'd never had a single conversation with any of the women he'd brought here. Only sex. Which he could have already had with her—if he'd pushed it.

"Am I?"

She went still beneath his silent stare. Her voice lowered

to a scratchy whisper. "Too good. You make me feel like I belong...like I'm special."

Her compliment stung, maybe because that's the way she made him feel.

"Maybe you are."

She got up stiffly and took her plate to the sink. When she sat back down and sipped her coffee, she seemed pale. The banana leaves were still now, the wind outside having died. The tiny kitchen got so quiet all he could hear was his own heart.

She was a stranger, but her sensual, feminine presence charged him. His uneasiness grew. Maybe that was why he got up and washed dishes with such a boisterous clatter. When he was done, he grabbed a bottle of whiskey and sat down, splashing a shot into his coffee. "Want some?"

She caught her lower lip nervously in her teeth, then shook her head.

Small talk. What to say when he couldn't think. When he was too damned conscious of *that* body, of the warmth of that silky skin, of the softness and sweetness of those red lips. His desire for her was a pulsing, tangible want. Not like what he'd felt for the others.

Small talk. With a woman he'd seen naked but whose mind was a stranger to him. "So, how come you talk to your mirror, pretty lady?"

"You shouldn't have spied on me."

He swallowed his whiskey, not liking the way it burned going down. "That's beside the point. Why do you talk to yourself?"

"You don't give up."

He stared at her ruby-red lips as she sipped from her cup and then set it crookedly in its saucer.

"I shouldn't tell," she began, hypnotizing him with her gaze.

"Oh, go ahead. We're both living dangerously tonight," he said.

"I was a shy, unpopular child. I used to read...all the time...and the things that happened in my books were so exciting. When I was a little girl I used to sit in front of my mirror and drape myself with scarves. I'd put on makeup...preen. My sister used to accuse me of being vain and conceited. But I was pretending I was in some exotic locale like the ones I read about. I was always with a pirate or a bandit...doing forbidden, adventurous things."

"So you like pirates?" He poured more whiskey into his cup.

Her lips pursed as she stared at the cup. At him. Then she got up so fast she nearly knocked her chair over.

"Hey...hey...."

Recovering, she walked away from him down the long hallway that led to his den. She eyed his bookshelves with a maddening nonchalance that challenged him, fingering his books, the stacks of real estate and investment magazines, learning about him without asking, when he didn't know a damn thing about her.

"I don't know any pirates," she finally said.

"You know me."

"I don't want to talk about this. Not to you." Deftly she changed the subject. "Your house is surprisingly neat."

His mouth twisted. "You mean for a low-life like me."

"I didn't say that." She paused and straightened the frame of a wild seascape that included a shrimp boat and a stormy sky swirling with gulls. "I like this painting."

"There's a lot of local talent here."

"Everything fits somehow. I mean your house. It's simple and comfortable. Classy...not overdone."

"What'd you expect?"

"Not this." She sounded a little disappointed. "I thought you'd be wild."

"Hey, I'm not all that neat...or tame." He threw back his head and drained his cup. Then almost angrily he flung the empty cup into a corner, smashing it to bits.

She gazed at him, her face shocked. "What'd you go and do that for?"

He grabbed for her, but she jumped, eluding him.

"Simmer down," he whispered. "That was just to prove...I've got a wild side. As for my neat house," he began, still on the defensive. "I have some help. A lady and her kid live in the house out back. Cute kid. Kinda nosey sometimes. But cute."

She ran down the length of the hall, vanishing into his den. "More bookshelves. You must read an awful lot."

He followed her. "Lots of lonely people read. It was a habit I started as a kid. There was a nice lady at the school library. I didn't know many nice ladies."

She was staring at him again, making him breathe too hard.

"So," he continued, "you dreamed about pirates because they...were exciting?"

"I'd rather talk about you."

"Fine," he said.

"What's your favorite book?"

"Whatever book I'm currently reading. I read nonfiction, mainly biographies. I don't like novels. They're..."

"Too emotional," she finished.

"Maybe. Now it's your turn. What's your favorite book?"

"*Frenchman's Creek*. It's a novel."

"About pirates?"

"How—" She blushed. "A married lady does have an adventure with a pirate."

"Does she choose the pirate or her husband?"

She was standing by the screen door, watching him.

"Her heart chooses the pirate, but she stays with her husband."

He moved toward her, closing in, cornering her. "That's not very romantic." He kept walking till he had her backed against the door.

"Oh, it was…in the book," she breathed, clutching the door.

He was so close he could feel the heat of her body and catch her sweet, feminine scent. "So, she had a fling?"

Her gaze seized on his carved face with fear and silent longing. "Your eyes are the coolest gray and yet…they burn…like no other eyes I've ever seen." She shuddered. "I bet no pirate ever had hotter eyes…."

He assumed a hard, insolent expression. *Girl, don't you be thinking what you're thinking. Fantasies are dangerous in real life.*

Shaking her head, she pushed the screen door open behind her and stepped out onto the breezeway. He followed close on her heels, the door clapping shut behind him, the sound that of summers and childhoods and memories buried deep but never forgotten. When she stepped onto the porch and climbed down to the lawn, he was right behind her. The night smelled of wet grass and salt air, and he could hear the gentle lapping of the surf beyond.

Not far from the house, she stopped and stared out at his hammock beneath the trees, at the wharf where his favorite shrimp boat was docked and then at the bay that stretched toward a moon-bright horizon.

"It's pretty out here…. I like the way your oak trees bent almost double from the wind. I like the way moonlight sparkles all the way across the bay."

"I don't think there's any other place quite like Rockport, but I never realized how gorgeous it all was before." He wasn't one for views, so he didn't stare at the familiar bay that hid sunken oyster reefs or the sculpted trees all the local artists painted so often; his devouring gaze raked the length of her.

Shakily she began to button the collar of her shirt. She was so golden and slender and lush and lovely. So uncertain and at the same time, so blatantly seductive.

"Black's damn sure your color, sweetheart," he drawled, repeating himself. His eyes shone. He wanted to seize her, to hold her, to crush her into his body, to taste her again, but she stiffened and backed away.

Music drifted toward them from Shorty's, Frenchy's favorite honky-tonk down the road.

"I like that song," she said.

Frenchy? Was he still meddling?

"I feel like dancing," Tag murmured gently. "How about you, pretty lady?"

"What? Here?"

"Play like I'm your fantasy pirate." He held out his hand and bowed low, inviting her to dance on his lawn beneath twisted oaks and silvery moonlight. Her soft gaze locked on his outstretched hand, then on his rugged, dark face, and last of all, she was drawn to his eyes that were aglow with passionate tenderness.

He hardly dared hope that the scene would appeal to that wild romantic imagination of hers and was stunned when her expression became drowsy and voluptuous. Then her cheeks reddened, but she laid her warm fingers over his. He slid his arm around her waist and drew her close.

Soon they were swaying in perfect harmony to the beat of the music. When she laid her cheek against his shoulder, his heart raced.

"So...what's your name?" he asked lightly.

"No names."

"We've shared violence, a bed, a meal, coffee...." He could feel her heartbeats quickening. "You're in my arms—"

"No names," she insisted, drawing a long breath. "They're too personal. This is a dream. Only a dream."

"Miss *X?*" He tipped his head back and stared thoughtfully at her pink face. "I guess that makes me Captain *X.* Same last name. Sounds like we're married."

She shivered and fought to pull away, but the music grew louder. And his arms tightened around her, holding her closer, so close that every time he moved, her legs and thighs burned his so intimately, waves of heat lit every nerve.

Hesitantly, shyly, she laughed.

"No way could you end up married to a guy like me in real life," he whispered into her hair, kissing her scalp again.

Her voice was low and sad. "No way."

"But in your imagination you fall for bandits and pirates."

"I shouldn't have told you that."

"Doesn't anybody know who you really are and what turns you on?"

"Nice girls don't talk about such things."

"Not even to their boyfriends?"

She was silent.

Tag stopped dancing and pulled her deeper into the shadows. "How come you're telling them to me tonight, instead of to him?" he demanded.

"We quarreled." She tossed her head. "It was silly really."

"But it changed everything."

"What do you mean?"

"I mean Rusty...Hank. That alley. I mean your torn dress, that lump on your head. I mean.... Tonight. Fate. You. Me. *Us.*"

"There is no...*us*—"

"So you'll go home and pretend you never met me."

She pressed her cheek to his chest again. "I have to. My life is perfect."

His eyes blazed, intent on her lips. "On the surface maybe."

He moved so swiftly she had no chance to evade him. The first thing she felt was the warmth of his breath against her cheek. Then his mouth covered hers. Almost instantly her eyelids closed and her breath caught expectantly.

Before she could surrender, he released her shoulders and pulled back. "How come you melt every time I touch you?"

"Don't— Please—"

"Sweetheart, it's real easy to think a life that measures up outwardly is the life you want. It's what everybody in this country thinks. You can have the great husband, the great house, the great car, but if those images are false, they won't matter any more than a new toy to a spoiled child. Someday, I swear to you, you'll find yourself out in the cold—alone...feeling empty...and all used up. I know—" He caught himself. "Sorry. I got carried away."

"Don't apologize." She turned her face fully toward him. Her eyes had softened with some intense emotion. "What is it about you...." There was awe in her voice. She drew a long, agonized breath that held pure feeling. "Why, oh, why...why do I feel..." She broke off, almost hurled herself back into his arms. "Just dance with me. Hold me," she begged. "Do you want to hear something crazy? I know I should run. Right now. This very minute. At the same time I wish this night could last forever."

"I learned you can't count on anything, and there's no such thing as forever. There's only now. This instant. You. Me. If it's good—go for it." Her heat consumed him. Her innocent smell was dizzying.

He pulled her close, whirled her across the lawn. She

glided, laughing now. He wanted to crush her to him, to kiss her, carry her into his bedroom.

He felt the heat of her body, the softness of her breasts. Then she stumbled, fell against him. He caught her and held her, his hands moving down her shoulders to her waist. He pressed her tighter. When the song ended, the mood between them was electric.

The sea breezes ruffled the leaves in the oak trees. Strands of her hair came loose and flew against his cheek. An odd shiver went through them both.

"Kiss me," she whispered, hardly breathing.

"What about your real life? Tomorrow?"

"What am I going to do? I have this thing for pirates who carry me away to a desert isle." Her eyes were startlingly blue, drinking in his soul. "You said I couldn't leave...not till the sun comes up. You said— Never mind what you said. Just kiss me...."

Intending a swift, light kiss, Tag cupped her face in his hands. Maybe she was inexperienced, but she was starving. Looping her arms around his neck, she nudged her tongue inside the moist aperture of his lips, kissing him back too hungrily for a tender peck to do.

Her hands. Her burning hands were all over him. She was an innocent, untutored, but her fumbling explorations, her natural wantonness stirred him more than all his previous, more experienced lovers had. And yet there was something clean and pure and true in every thing she did. She was everything he'd dreamed of that could be good in life and more.

Liquid heat spiraled through him. A low moan rose from his throat. She pulled back, moonlight streaming across her pale, stunned face. Her cheeks were flushed, her mouth swollen as she began to unbutton her black shirt.

He ran his fingers through his hair, gulped in air as she

stripped. Whipping his shirt off, she stood before him, her opulent breasts gleaming in the silver light.

"Tell me who you are," he whispered.

"No names."

So—she was…like the others.

She tossed him the shirt and ran. He chased her through the high grasses, into the deepening shadows of the trees.

He pounced when she came out of the thicket at the back of the house. Picking her up, he carried her to the house. Inside, he pressed her against the wall. With his free hand, he slowly stroked her warm neck, her shoulders, her breasts. "Don't make me stop," he growled.

"Oh…oh," she whispered in a small, frightened voice when his fingers rubbed her nipples till they hardened. Then he suckled first one and then the other.

Her eyes were torpid and unfocused. "Please…oh… please…."

"Please…what?"

"I…I…I'm too ashamed to ask."

He lifted his head.

"And too filled with delight not to ask." A sheen of tears glazed her eyes. "Would you pretend—"

"Anything—" he murmured hoarsely, recklessly.

"Would you be…my midnight fantasy? Would you play the pirate I sometimes dream about?"

"Loverboy?" he whispered.

There was something so needy and vulnerable, so imploring in her guilt-stricken blue gaze when she nodded. She made him burn and ache as no woman ever had before.

His large hands plunged into her hair. He tugged the rubberband loose, and yellow hair spilled to her shoulders. She cried out in pain at first but then began to shiver when he ran his fingers through the long perfumed masses before burying his hot mouth beneath them, first hungrily kissing her throat and then lowering his mouth to taste again her nipples that were still wet and taut from his previous kisses. His hands parted the zipper of her jeans, but her hands rushed to stop him. He got down on his knees, cupped her buttocks, pulled her pelvis against his face. His warm breath teased denim that covered that most erogenous of feminine places. Instantly her hands were in his black hair and she was shuddering.

"So, my pretty, nameless virgin, you want to be ravished, do you?" he whispered.

Five

Ravished?

Claire's blue eyes darkened with incredulity and disgust as she stared at the trampy looking girl with the frizzy blond hair and the purple hickey on her neck in *his* bathroom mirror. She could still taste him thrillingly on her swollen lips just as she could taste, smell, and sense disaster awaiting her in his house.

Her fists clenched as she eyed her reflection. "I don't know you! I don't want to know you!"

You want it. You need it—bad.

Loverboy's silken, silent taunt in her head.

"No!"

"I hear you," Loverboy's real-life, virile counterpart thundered from the other side of the thin, bathroom door. "You're talking to yourself again, Sugar-Baby!"

Sugar-Baby. Loverboy. They weren't real.

But he was.

Head throbbing, she sagged against the wall. How could this be happening? She couldn't hurt North after what he'd been through. She and North were the perfect couple. Everybody said so. He was the catch of south Texas. She was madly, madly in love with him.

Wasn't she? When she tried to think of North's dear, handsome face, instead, the image of a battered warrior's transfixed her. Merciless gray eyes, eyes as pale as the silver moon pinned her, claimed her soul, made every nerve buzz with sweet longing. The dream they shared was all-powerful.

How deliciously warm *his* long body had felt next to hers under his sheet. His mouth on her breasts had sent jolts of blind, carnal sensation through every part of her. And she was still on fire and aching for more of the same. Why did she feel her whole life had meant nothing till him?

A wave of dizziness swamped her. The lump on her head. That had to be why. Why she wasn't herself. Why she was in this mess. Spellbound.

She had to get out of here! Away from him! She had to break this blasted connection to a man who was utterly and completely wrong! Before he destroyed her whole life!

She touched the telltale bruises on her throat. They would be impossible to explain to North or her mother. This man had kissed her so deeply, consumed her almost…made her knees go so weak, he'd had to pick her up. After he'd carried her inside, he'd put on music that matched his mood. They'd danced and danced, their bodies moving as if they were one.

Now the CD thrummed faster than the wildest voodoo drums, and her own heart was pounding even faster.

Something crashed against his bedroom wall. What was he doing? On a shudder she backed against the door.

How could she get away from him? When every time she looked at him, she sensed his inner pain, his masculine need of her and was thrilled on some primal, female level. He turned her on, made her melt, made her feel utterly new and whole, made her feel that she belonged with him forever. Which was crazy. It was as if he were everything, and her real life, all her ambitions, her friends, her family, were nothing. As if this dream was real and lasting.

She had to get out of here. Make some excuse. No. She didn't dare talk to him.

Then what?

His bike was still at the mechanic's. If she could just get to her car, get it started, before he realized she was gone.... Maybe she'd have a chance.

When his hard knuckles rapped impatiently on the door, she nearly jumped out of her skin.

"I need to come in there."

"What for?" When he hesitated, she said, "Don't you have another bathroom?"

"Okay. But I'm done with the costume. I wanted you to see it."

"I'm sure it's great," she whispered.

"I even painted on a moustache."

"I...I can't wait...."

"Hurry." His retreating footsteps thudded heavily down the hall. A door slammed at the other end of the house.

This was her chance! When she tried to push the door open and peer out, hinges groaned loud enough to wake a corpse. Which sent her rushing noisily down the hall, careening down the steps of the porch, flying toward the garage and carport. She leapt into her car, slammed the door, and grabbed wildly for the keys.

They weren't there!

She almost wept. "Where?" she sobbed. "Where?" She fumbled under the floormat. Then she looked up and the constellation Scorpio danced above her.

"Where?"

"Right here, Sugar-Baby." His deep, gravelly voice made the skin on the back of her neck prickle. Keys jingled high above her head. She blanched when they disappeared in the high grasses behind his house. She'd never find them, never get away. She kept a spare set chained under her bumper, but there was no way she could get them now.

He yanked her door open and bowed low. "I thought you wanted to play pirate," he jeered, holding out his hand to help her alight.

She studied those long, lean fingers with the shading of hair at the center and felt her stomach go weightless. She swallowed. "Not anymore."

"You mean...not with me." His silken voice turned her blood to ice.

Moonlight streamed across his dark skin, across the carved angles of his brutal face, across the evil-looking moustache he had painted on. He ripped off the black patch that covered one eye and threw it to the ground. "Nobody plays me for a fool. Not even you—Miss *X*."

A strong blue vein throbbed in his throat. His gray eyes glittered. He was furious, close to some sheer edge.

"I'm sorry," she said thickly. "You obviously took a lot of pains with your costume."

His black gaze skewered her. "To please you, damn it."

He wore a loose, long-sleeved, white cotton shirt that was unbuttoned from his neck to his lean waist. Skin-tight denim molded his powerful, muscular legs. He'd even slashed the bottom edges of his jeans to look like pirate garb, and his brown feet were bare. From somewhere he'd found a red sash and tied it around his waist. A gold chain and coin glittered against the mat of black curling hair that shadowed his broad chest. His silver earring glinted from beneath the red kerchief that bound his ebony hair.

Loverboy. The pirate lover of her dreams. In warm, sun-bronzed flesh. With blazing silver eyes. Somehow he was more handsome than she'd ever imagined, more compelling, too.

She knelt and picked up the black patch. "I am sorry I put you to so much trouble."

"The prize I intend to claim makes it worth it." Erotic danger put a roughness in his low tone, added more fire to the intense silver eyes that raked her.

"I underestimated you."

"Likewise," he replied.

"You're angry. I know you feel rejected."

"You don't know me at all."

"Which is the problem—"

"Why did I think you were different? You want to play the same tired game. You wanted a fling…with the forbidden…with some rough-cut, low-class stranger the real you despises…before you tie yourself to your fancy, boring life and statusy man forever. You were using me."

"I'm-m s-sorry," she stammered

"You started this, sweetheart. But do you have the guts to finish it?" He seized her, his lips smothering hers almost violently.

Why was it so impossible to fight him? Her arms twined around his neck. When his tongue dipped inside her mouth, her tongue met his so eagerly he groaned aloud and then threw her from him.

"Go," he muttered, his voice savage, his eyes dark, almost agonized. "Go…before I change my mind."

But his kiss had started something that had to be finished.

"Don't be hurt—"

"To hell with you! Go home. Quickly. To your fancy boyfriend…. Go…before…something happens tonight we both regret."

She licked her lips, tasted him, and that only made her want him more. "You would regret it, too?"

"Does that surprise you?" he demanded. "That I'm not

all animal? That I might feel something? That I might attach some emotion other than lust to our little sexual encounter? You think you're so superior to me. I know your kind. Go home. Leave me be. I'm sick and tired of women like you—women who come looking for cheap thrills but who could care less about…'' He stopped abruptly.

Why did he sound almost injured…almost jealous…and angry, too? Even more angry at himself than he was at her? And so desolate and lonely?

Pirate costume or no, he was a real human being. Not some fantasy of her own imagination. Not somebody to use or tease for a night's pleasure. He wasn't a dream. He was real….

He'd dressed up for her.

Because he'd wanted to please her.

He made her feel special. For the first time in her life.

Don't listen to him. He did it for sex. He couldn't care about her…any more than she could let herself care about him.

North hadn't followed her from the party. This man had followed her into a dark alley and fought two thugs for her. It had been one against two. They could've been armed, but he'd fought for her anyway, had saved her life, risked his own life to do it. Then he'd seen to the repairs of her car, comforted her when she wept with belated hysteria, taken her home, protected her. She'd been so scared. He was tough, but nobody had ever made her feel so gently protected, so precious, so tenderly cared for as he did. And even angry, he did look darling in that costume.

Beneath his temper, there was genuine concern. He was scowling, yet she felt a melting sweetness inside her. She longed for more of his kisses, for his touch. For everything.

Which was insane.

Dazed, she stared at his dark, angry face in confusion, not knowing what to do.

He shrugged in disgust. Then he turned his back on her and walked away.

If he'd slapped her, he couldn't have made her feel more rejected.

Her heart and soul leapt with lightning speed. Then a still quiet voice inside her told her what to do.

Claire had no idea her life had changed course. Tomorrow the voices of family, duty, and grave self-doubt would scream louder than her heart. Tonight that still, quiet part of her knew that from the moment she'd met this man, he'd become everything.

Now he was walking away, and she couldn't bear it.

"No," she cried.

He kept walking.

Without knowing what she did or why, she started after him, slowly at first. Then she was running, hurling herself after his broad-shouldered form. Arms wrapping around him, she hugged him, pressing her face into his spine.

He turned slowly, read her beautiful face. In his eyes, did she only imagine she saw hope and joy as well as profound self-doubt and melting pain?

Breathless, her heart beating thunderously, she stood very still. Their gazes burned.

After a long moment his slow grin lit her whole being. "Make up your mind, sweetheart," he commanded in that low, hard voice she already loved.

When she flung her arms around him, he buried his face in her neck, his breath warm against her satin skin.

"This is scary for me, too," he whispered thickly against her hair. "Everybody I've ever cared for has left me. Even I…left me. I've been dead. I wanted to be dead. But you… *You. Why?*"

He began to kiss her, his lips, loving and gentle and yet hard, too.

Everything he did, everything he said, filled her with

yearning and made her forget all thoughts of wrong. Then
he picked her up, swirled her round and round so that her
golden hair was flying. Slowing, he stopped spinning and
held her high above his black head. Just as slowly he lowered her so that every delicious inch of her body slid against
his face, his lips.

Adrift in pleasure, her fingers curved around his neck,
curled into the long, thick black hair at his nape.

"You're sure? Very sure?" he demanded in a raw, ur-
gent tone.

She nodded.

He ran the back of his knuckles down her cheek. "You
are beautiful. Exquisite. You make me come alive."

His next kiss was different, harder, more insistent with
purpose and yet softer, holding infinite wonder. His hands
moved over her, caressing her hair, her throat, every part
of her. They slid under her shirt. Then he buried his face
in her breasts, hugged her close, and sighed as if releasing
some deep, bitter pain.

"Time to play pirate," he teased a long time later. More
kisses followed, but these were playful. When they were
both breathless, he dragged her eagerly across the grasses,
to the wharf, to his boat.

He lifted her on board and began casting off lines. Soon
the boat was drifting away from the dock, out into the
moonlit bay.

"What are you doing?"

He ducked inside the pilothouse. "I'm a pirate abducting
my pretty lady."

"This is a shrimp boat. You're a shrimper."

"...among other trades...." His voice had darkened.
"You might be surprised.... But who are you—underneath?"

"I...I don't want to talk about myself."

"You want to play dangerous games. Let me guess. Soft

hands. Soft skin. Silky hair. Life's been very good to you. Money. Class. You don't have to work."

"I work very, very hard."

"Book work which is easy for you because you're smart."

"How would you know?"

"You're a reader."

"When I have time," she admitted. "You've probably been to good schools."

"The best," she said quietly.

"And you think me a poor, illiterate shrimper."

"You read."

His eyes held secrets. "You think I'm beneath you. Not good enough for a lady like you." He touched her, ran his hands boldly down her breasts, staking his claim before yanking her close. "Except for this," he said, his lethal gaze disconcertingly direct. "Sex. I'm good enough for *this.*"

"*This?*"

His rough hands were inside her shirt, all over her breasts. Her spine went taut as one hand flowed downward. "Us." His mouth was on hers. "Tonight. You and me."

"I don't understand."

"You don't want to. Lots of girls go slumming for thrills."

"Not me."

"Guys do the same thing." He made some quick adjustment with the engine and put the boat on autopilot. "But who am I to judge? You want to hear something funny? I want you to be different. Me to be different. *This* to be special."

What he said scared her, but before she could protest, he seized her, tossing her over his wide shoulder.

Kicking, her head lightly bouncing upside down against his spine, she screamed.

"Put me down!"

"You started this game."

Stomping swiftly down the stairs, he flung her gently onto his narrow bunk. She was scrambling to escape him when he grabbed her ankle and yanked her back.

"Me illiterate pirate. You fair, civilized lady." He thumped his chest which was as hard as iron. "Maybe tomorrow night we'll swing from the oak trees and play Tarzan and Jane." At her look of shock, he laughed. "Oh, I know, I know. There won't be a tomorrow. You want me to kiss you, get it over with—"

She squeezed her eyes shut and took a deep breath. That wasn't really what she wanted—

He seized her, kissed her, his heavy body tumbling on top of her, his dominant position making it easy to hold her down. She wanted to explain, so she kicked and squirmed as he unzipped her jeans, shoved them down her thighs.

Then his hand dipped into her.

Whatever she would have said to defend herself died on her lips. She went still in shock, but then began to tremble with pleasure. She squeezed her eyes shut, twisting away from him shyly and yet clasping him, too.

"You're so tight."

"I—I'm a virgin."

He hesitated. "There has to be a first time," he said quietly. "Do you want it to be me?"

She looked at him. Strangely, she did.

Why? She studied his dark face. Then she nodded. She didn't know why. She didn't care why. It simply was.

When his fingers encountered resistance, he pushed, stroking gently until she grew wetter and began to moan. In seconds he was past the barrier and he had her gasping and arching up to his palm, writhing, crying out, begging him to take her.

His fingers plunged. Deeply. Inside.

"Us."

She cried out at the exquisite pressure and yet felt a completion to be touched there.

He stopped and waited. Only when she begged him, did he continue. It wasn't long till pain became pleasure, and she went up in flames.

He grinned. "Me. You."

All too soon his low voice and caressing, expert fingers were too erotic for words. He sensed every nuance of response in her, stopping time and again, taking her just to the edge of satiation. *"Us."*

His eyes held hers. His finger stayed inside her. "Say it," he commanded. "Say *us.*"

"Us," she repeated weakly, reveling in the intimacy of his touch and words.

His mouth stretched into a slow, triumphant grin. With a deft flick, his hand moved, and she exploded.

He let her rest. Then he ripped off his sash and blindfolded her.

She fingered the red silk that covered her eyes. "Why?" she whispered, afraid.

"Trust me."

She felt shaky, shy, unsure.

"Trust yourself. You've wanted this for years," he said. "If you hadn't met me, you might have lived your whole life without it."

No. She didn't want it. Or just sex. It was him she wanted.

"Now imagine you're on a pirate ship, its hold full of gold. I'm the pirate captain, and my sheets are red satin. You're my captive, my slave, part of my booty, and you have to please me or I'll give you to my men. Not really, for I have a jealous nature, and I covet you too much to

ever follow through…but you don't know that. You think
you must please me, or I'll sell you to the highest bidder."

Her stomach knotted on a strange thrill.

"Strip, my lady." His low-pitched, hard voice made her
shiver and go hot all over. "Slowly."

Loverboy's words.

"Strip, I said."

A helpless feeling of inevitability possessed her. Somehow this man knew all her secret and most wanton desires.

She swallowed against the dry, hot lump in her throat
and clumsily began unbuttoning the black cotton shirt he
had loaned her. She heard his low groan of pleasure when
she eased it over her shoulders, off her breasts and let it
fall. For an instant or two she just lay there blushing because she didn't know where his eyes were and yet she
could sense his excitement as they burned down her throat,
her nipples, her navel.

Hurriedly, because she felt shy and unsure, she began
pushing her jeans further down, and then curled into a fetal
ball, trying to hide herself.

"No," he growled. "Go slower. Stretch out…full
length…like a cat in heat. Purr. Beg. Seduce…but make
me wait."

"I…I can't."

"Tantalize me."

"How?"

"You're a woman. And beautiful. Move. Undulate. Run
your hand down your body. Open your legs."

Shyly she curled her body into his and then bent one
knee.

"Take my hand, sweetheart. Put it where you most want
to be touched. Use it as you would…to pleasure yourself."

"I…"

"Sex is more fun than anything else…if you let yourself
go."

If you're with the right man.

Some other force outside herself took his hand and put it beneath her knee so that he could run his hands up the inside of her thigh. Soon she was arching up to meet his caresses as he trailed lips and fingers everywhere.

"Kiss me," she whispered.

With his tongue, he suckled her breasts. Then he hooked his thumbs around the elastic of her thong bikini panties and peeled them down her long legs. "Now strip me, pretty lady," he said in that playful, harsh tone.

Because she couldn't see him, this was much more difficult. Blindly, she climbed on top him, straddling his lean waist. She swayed over him, her golden hair swinging loosely over his chest. He caught her wrist, blew a warm kiss into her palm that sent a tremor through her.

For no reason, the urge to trace her fingertips along his nose and brow seized her. Blindly she used both hands to learn with her fingertips the dark, carved beauty of his male features. It was a long time before she scooted her pelvis lower. Then her trembling hands trailed down his neck, down his torso to grasp the bottom edges of his shirt.

"Peel it off. Kiss me," he whispered, his breathing ragged now. Inch by inch, she pushed the white cotton back, trailing her lips upward over his lean, naked torso, then his furry chest.

"Unzip me."

She hesitated.

"Don't think. Just do it." He grabbed her hand, and she obeyed helplessly, not because he forced her, but because she wanted to. When she had him unzipped, he urged her to reach inside and touch him as he had touched her earlier, and when she did, that started everything.

In a microsecond he was on fire; in the next so was she. He paused just long enough to dig a condom out of a drawer and put it on. Then he rolled over, covering her completely. He pressed his tongue inside her mouth at the same moment his hips thrust deeply. She would have cried out, but his mouth smothered hers with kisses. He undid the blindfold. He began to move, thrusting again and again inside her, and each time he did, she felt more intimately joined, more completely, thrillingly his. He took her higher and higher into their dark whirling fantasy that was so much more wonderful and meaningful than her wildest dream. Crushed beneath him, she felt his arms wrapped tightly around her. Time and again he plunged, until finally he lost himself and all the dark desperation in his soul shattered on a tidal wave of desire for her.

When it was over, she lay in his arms, too shaken to move.

Sex.

Not just sex.

"Us," he had said.

He had claimed every part of her.

She regarded him shyly.

His dark gaze was even warier than hers, and his voice was infinitely changed. "I told you these are dangerous games, my lady."

"Why did this happen?"

He fingered the damp tendrils that were glued to her brow. "It's easy to become addicted to such pleasurable experiences. One or both of us might not want them to end."

"Every game has to end."

"If indeed, it's a game." He paused. "Love's a wild-card."

"Love?" she whispered softly.

"Sex then. Lust. Cupid's mischievous arrow. This. Us. Call it what you like. A night like tonight can change everything. Winner take all."

She turned her face away. "Lust and love—they're the same to you?"

He stroked his knuckles down the length of her spine. "When a man gets lucky."

"Like tonight?" she whispered.

His voice was suddenly dark, lost. "I thought I was playing a bad hand tonight. Then you came along."

"What do you mean?"

"Once I was good at games. The stakes were high—like tonight. But I was a winner—always...till the last hand. When I lost, I lost big. You're not the only one with secrets, my love."

My love. The endearment lit her soul.

He began to kiss her, and all too soon she was trembling, protesting, sighing, and then succumbing to the magic again.

The second session was sweeter, wilder. It lasted longer. When it was over, they were too awed for words. But he stayed inside her and held her until she fell sound asleep.

She awoke some time in the night, every muscle in her body aching, but her heart more joyous than ever before. The beach house was awash in moonlight. Their bodies were joined, their arms and legs tangled in boneless contentment.

She had been dreaming her recurring dream of being wrapped in colored banners of silk.

"Unwrap me, Loverboy," she'd teased.

On their way back from the boat, they'd waded in warm, ankle-deep water, picked up feathers and shells. In his bed, she'd run a feather over his torso while his pale eyes raked her hotly as she drove him wild. He'd returned the favor, only he'd used it with far more skill than she.

Flushing in embarrassment, she relived everything she'd done, everything he'd done, every look, every wanton touch they'd shared. At the end, she'd been moved to tears,

tears of joy and tears of the loss she felt at the thought of not seeing him again. He made promises, such sweet promises, promises she couldn't let him keep.

When she glanced down at the floor, his pirate costume, the clothes he'd loaned her, as well as the feathers and silver shells littered the floor. Her soulful eyes studied him.

If he woke up, what would he say? Do? Want?

She was afraid of all she might want, so she forced herself to thoughts that cheapened what they'd shared.

What did a night like that make her? Was he right when he'd said she was no better than other girls seeking a fleeting thrill from a rough guy who was good in bed?

What did it matter what he thought? She had to put this incredible, this inexplicable night, *him,* all her longings, his passionate promises and understanding of her, behind her.

Only this morning she had her whole life figured out. She was getting married, going to medical school…. There was North. And her mother. She couldn't hurt them the way Melody had.

But, if she didn't get out of here and fast, she would. Some deep instinct told her, this man wanted her on a level more profound than anyone would ever want her, that all he might have to do was touch her to keep her.

Still, for a while she lay in his arms, savoring the warmth of his steady breath in her hair. Tears formed on her lashes. It was so pleasant lying here with him. So dangerously pleasant to recall all the strange and wonderful intimacies they'd shared.

Then he murmured an endearment, reminding her she couldn't risk his waking and finding her. Easing herself out of his arms, she dressed hurriedly.

But at the door she made the fatal mistake of turning to look at him. His male beauty stopped her dead. That final glance at his rumpled dark head, his lithe, bronze body, was all it took to make her heartbeats accelerate with fresh stabs of pain.

When she saw the feathers and shells and his black eye patch on the floor, she started shaking. With a muffled sniffle, she leaned down, picked up his eye patch, one feather and a seashell. Each treasure, she pressed to her lips.

When she stood up to go, tears began to cascade down her cheeks. Maybe that was why she didn't notice her change purse falling out of her handbag.

He made a sound, reached for her, and she fled swiftly down the hall.

Six

Tag awoke to the jaunty roar of her sports car and the squeal of tires bouncing off the curb of his driveway. Queasily, he shot to a sitting position just as a red car zoomed out of his carport and vanished down the road.

The cotton sheet he yanked back was cool to his touch. Her side of the bed was empty.

Her absence struck him like a blow. For a moment he couldn't breathe.

Good. He forced that thought. *She was gone!*

Like his mother. Like his father. Like the women who came to the bar and used him for sex.

For no particular reason his heart thudded so violently he thought it might implode.

Which was absurd. He hardly knew her. The last thing he'd expected or wanted was a fairy tale.

But she'd been so sweet. The sheets he'd brought home from his boat were spotted with her blood. He remembered how she'd clung to him at the end, how she'd wept, great wrenching sobs...because she'd explained, threading her hands through his hair, pulling his face down to hers. Because she'd loved what they'd done together more than she could ever express in words.

"I'm crying because it was so beautiful, so perfect.... Because I adore you."

Adore. That word, the sweet way she'd said it, with that look of utter vulnerability softening her fragile features had set off a furor inside him.

She wasn't like the others.

"Because you make me whole," she'd whispered, her luminous eyes burning him. "Because I can't ever see you again."

Words said during sex weren't to be believed. Still, he couldn't forget what she'd said. He'd said equally tender things to her.

"It doesn't have to be like that." He'd cradled her against himself, his arms wrapping her, believing in that moment he could protect her from all pain. "I care about you."

Her tear-glazed eyes had held his with a fervor so fierce, she'd mesmerized him. "If only—"

That was then—before the white-heat of their passion had slowed to a simmer. This was now—in the cold light of a new sun that blazed on the flat sea beyond his house.

"I'm not what you think," he'd whispered in that same nighttime voice and mood. "Tell me who you are."

"Shhh." She cupped his carved face as if he were very dear, put a finger to his lips. Then she'd kissed the edges of his mouth, the tip of his nose, his brow. Finally, she'd laid her soft cheek against his and snuggled so close to his body, he'd been totally enveloped by the perfumed warmth of her legs and arms.

Exhausted, not wanting to let her go, he'd fallen asleep in her arms.

But she was gone. Nameless like all the others.

They were adults. They would pick up and go on as if last night hadn't happened. She'd given him something to brag about the next time he got drunk.

As if he'd share her, in any way, with those bastards at Shorty's.

She'd been a virgin.

He'd been her first.

Which meant nothing.

Which did.

Tag combed his hands through his mussed black hair. He told himself he wasn't straining to hear her car long after it was gone. He told himself he wasn't listening to the gulls soaring beyond the trees.

Trousers nudged the door open with his nose, padded across the floor and laid his head on the bed and stared at him with hungry, glowing eyes. Which meant it was time for breakfast.

"Damn it!" Tag felt too lethargic to get up and get on with his day. He laid a hand on the warm fur. Trousers whined and began to lick his hand.

Old hurts rushed back, sharpened by the wisdom of his years. Tag remembered the wonder he'd felt when his father's wife had first led him into his charmingly furnished blue bedroom with its models of ships and armies of tin soldiers in New Orleans.

"Your father had me fix it up for you."

It had seemed like a dream. A dream he hadn't wanted to end even though he'd felt like a fraud.

Last night when she'd worn his clothes, praised his omelette, asked him to play pirate, he'd experienced that same young-again, bittersweet wonder that life could feel so good.

He hadn't wanted it to end.

"Who the hell was she, Trousers?"

Tail flicking, Trousers lay down on the floor to wait.

Wrap me. Unwrap me.

Blue eyes sparkling in the dark as she eagerly twirled round and round with the excitement of a playful little girl, pressing those pink shells over her breasts.

Strip, my lady. Slowly.

Tear-streaked eyes, a woman's eyes, memorizing his face right before she fell asleep in his arms.

Who the hell was this fantasy girl with the yellow hair who liked to dance and strip and make love with feathers? Who'd made him feel young again.

Who made him care. Who made him want to be a different man.

He'd wanted her. He'd taken her.

She'd willingly let him. End of story.

Despite her aura of class and money, she was no better than all his other cheap one-night stands.

She'd been a virgin.

It was over. So, forget her.

She'd gone back to her family.

When he saw the red scarf he'd used as a blindfold lying across the foot of the bed, he picked it up. The instant he touched it, he remembered undoing the knot, staring deeply into her eyes when he'd been inside her. And the memory of her sweet eagerness was a claw in his chest, tearing his heart out.

He felt nothing.

But he couldn't control his mind. Again he was in the cemetery on his bike, watching a girl with golden hair ride the wind. He saw her in the alley, half-naked…her eyes wide, terrified…. Those legs of hers that went for-damn-forever.

When Rusty had cut him, he'd been scared when blood

had gushed through his fingers. Scared they'd overpower him and hurt her. Scared they'd make her feel helpless and all alone, like he'd felt as a kid when the bullies had gotten him in back alleys behind his foster homes, when those thugs had nearly drowned him outside New Orleans.

But he'd kept her safe.

She'd been so beautiful. The way she'd looked at him. She'd been spooked...but spunky enough to stand up to him, too.

She was highbred, high-strung, ambitious. She was just like every other snob, who despised people who weren't like them. She'd made it painfully clear he couldn't be part of her life.

As he was going over every logical reason why he had to put her out of his mind, he saw her little black change purse on the floor a few feet from his bed. Groggily, he leaned down and snatched it.

The velvet was soft and elegant and sweet smelling...like the woman. Maybe her name or address was inside. Unzipping it, he shook out its contents.

A chill shot through him when a three-carat diamond engagement ring in a white gold, antique setting hit his palm. Eyes narrowing, he held the stone to the light in such a way that it seemed a faceted beacon emitting dazzling, fluttering bursts of white. She must've taken her ring off.

The brightness made him squint and caused hard lines to bracket his mouth. Sucking in a savage breath, Tag saw her in the arms of another, tamer man. This ring was a symbol of her attachment to that bright world that would never accept him.

His hand clenched on the rock so hard, a softer stone would have shattered.

What games would she play to get her diamond back? *Strip, my lady. Slowly.*

* * *

"Guilty conscience?" Melody's knowing smile was annoyingly cheerful when Claire stumbled into their mother's too-perfect kitchen in her trailing white nightgown and plopped wearily down on the stool opposite her sister.

"Guilty? About what?" Deliberately Claire kept her eyes downcast.

"What's with the ever-so-proper, Victorian nightgown? You look like you belong in another century with that high lace collar buttoned tight enough to choke you."

Claire pushed the prim lace ruffle higher. She'd worn the gown to hide her neck and because she knew the gown made her look virginal.

Which she never would be again.

Melody stared at Claire's pale features. Then she began to hum as was sometimes her habit. For some reason Melody reminded Claire of an unremorseful cat who'd swallowed a whole cage of canaries. Something was up with her.

Claire picked up a bridal magazine and began leafing through the glossy pages. White gowns. Wedding bouquets. She felt a drowning sorrow in her heart.

What had happened to the girl who'd believed—and not long ago—that such beautiful gowns were indeed magical, that her own wedding day would be wonderful, that she would make North and her mother very, very happy?

That girl had come blazingly alive in a forbidden stranger's arms. After that cornucopia of carnal pleasures, she might never be the same.

Claire forced herself to visualize herself frothily gowned in white lace, her train trailing the length of the sanctuary. But her imagination played a cruel trick on her, for it was the biker who dazzled her from the altar with a slow, heart-stopping grin—not North. She saw herself flying down the aisle, straight into her fantasy man's arms.

Dreams.

All her dreams had turned to dust.

A tear stung her lashes. She slammed the magazine shut. She looked up to sunlight filtering through massive French doors and brightening tile floors and chamois-colored walls and her mother's copper pots.

Dee Dee's elegant, fashionable kitchen seemed surreal. Claire shut her eyes, but that only made her conscious of the warring voices in her head.

"He means nothing."

"Liar."

"You won't forget him."

"I have."

"You're crazy about him."

"It was the bump on the head."

"Shouldn't you see him again…to make sure?"

"No."

"Afraid you'd change your mind—Sugar-Baby?"

Shut up. Shut up.

When the patio door slammed, Claire toppled from her stool. *"It's Mother!"* she squeaked

"So?" Melody whispered, watching Claire scramble back onto her stool.

"Hello!" Dee Dee's shrill voice rang from the hall. "Hello? Anybody up?"

Dee Dee had to be the perfect mother, the perfect hostess, the perfect wife. She had to have the perfect house. Thus, she arose early, especially when her girls were home for a visit. Even on such days, she was compulsive about walking and swimming before it got too warm or before her busy day got away from her.

Melody set her coffee mug down squarely on top of her mother's catalogues, house and garden magazines, bills and checkbook. "Seven-thirty." With an impish smile, Melody tossed her long honey-gold hair. "On the dot. Nothing's changed since we left home. You can set your watch by

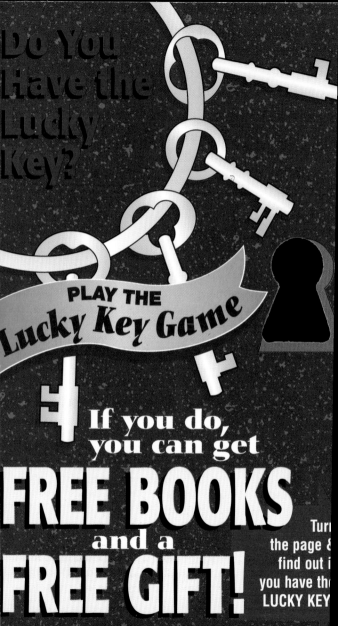

PLAY THE
Lucky Key Game and get

HOW TO PLAY:

1. With a coin, carefully scratch off gold area at the right. Then check the claim chart to see what we have for you — **2 FREE BOOKS** and a **FREE GIFT** — **ALL YOURS FREE!**

2. Send back the card and you'll receive two brand-new Silhouette Desire® novels. These books have a cover price of $3.99 each in the U.S. and $4.50 each in Canada, but they are yours to keep absolutely free.

3. There's no catch. You're under no obligation to buy anything. We charge nothing —ZERO — for your first shipment. And you don't have to make any minimum number of purchases — not even one!

4. The fact is, thousands of readers enjoy receiving books by mail from the Silhouette Reader Service™. They enjoy the convenience of home delivery...they like getting the best new novels at discount prices, BEFORE they're available in stores...and they love their *Heart to Heart* subscriber newsletter featuring author news, horoscopes, recipes, book reviews and much more!

5. We hope that after receiving your free books you'll want to remain a subscriber. But the choice is yours — to continue or cancel, any time at all! So why not take us up on our invitation, with no risk of any kind. You'll be glad you did!

YOURS FREE!
A SURPRISE MYSTERY GIFT

We can't tell you what it is...but we're sure you'll like it! A
FREE GIFT—
just for playing the
LUCKY KEY game!

Visit us online at
www.eHarlequin.com

Mother. And she's already got a half-dozen trucks in the front yard. Those men with the spiders are here. They're out there putting them in the trees. Yuck.''

Claire's heart wasn't in her smile. Only yesterday the thought of spiders and decorating for her wedding would have thrilled her.

The sisters were amazingly alike, and yet completely different. Both were slim, blond, and leggy. Both were bright overachievers. But while Claire was logical and reliable, Melody was intuitive and zanily impulsive. Claire was a dresser because she wanted to be admired. Melody reveled in the grunge look. This morning she wore a tattered, red football jersey that showcased her long, tawny legs. She wasn't wearing makeup, either. Still, in her own natural way, she was as beautiful as her stylish sister. Her sparkling smile made up for the lack of artifice and feminine wiles. And except for Dee Dee, who found Melody's flakiness unnerving, she was everybody's favorite, which was why, until last night, Claire had tried so hard.

Wearing a tight black swimsuit, Dee Dee whirled toward them like a human tornado. Her delicate blond looks and angelic smile masked a fierce will and temper. Baby, her devoted, snaggle-toothed Himalayan, was a fluffy white shadow chasing right behind her.

As always Dee Dee did at least three things at once. This morning while listening to a motivational tape, she'd watered her flower beds, completed her routine workout in her home gym, made lists for her maid and yard people, and then swum her usual number of laps in her swimming pool. Not to mention, she'd set in motion a project that was of uppermost importance to her—the spiders who were to spin webs in her trees.

Dee Dee had grown up in a crumbling plantation in Louisiana where tales were still told of a plantation wedding a hundred years ago. The father of the bride had imported spiders to spin webs in his oak trees. On the wedding day, he'd had gold glitter sprinkled into the trees, so that his trees had seemed to be draped in canopies of gold.

Dee Dee toweled herself off, unfurled the morning newspaper, set two new bridal magazines in front of Claire, eyed her to-do list, put out some fresh tuna for Baby, poured herself a cup of coffee, all while regarding both her daughters, especially Claire, avidly. Thanks to surgery, clothes, diet, genes, and an indulgent husband, Dee Dee hardly looked a day older than her girls.

Dee Dee frowned at Claire. "So, what's up with you two?"

Claire's tenuous smile fluttered. She pushed her high collar higher. "Nothing. I'm fine." Her voice sounded robotic, not hers at all.

Soon…soon she would regain her senses, and that little interlude with a nameless biker would make her even surer that her real world—her upper-middle-class parents, her sister, her acceptable friends, her academic record, her acceptances to top medical schools, even North—were the only things that could ever matter.

"You don't look well!"

"Bridal jitters," blurted Melody, who was her usual off-the-beam, intuitive self.

Claire swallowed. "Those spider men came so early. I'm…just a little tired."

Her heart wasn't threatening to explode, her burning eyes to flood. She didn't feel trapped or doomed in her mother's too-perfect house that somehow made all its occupants so edgy. She was thrilled to be home with her family again. Thrilled to be safe. Thrilled to be marrying North.

"But you're so pale, dear. There are dark shadows under your eyes. Have you been crying? You're not upset because your sister had that long talk with North last night, are you?"

"Melody? North?"

"I think it's wonderful they finally discussed—" Dee Dee noticed Claire's pallor and went quiet. "You're not jealous—"

"Mother!" said Melody.

"Melody was with North?" whispered Claire.

"When you ran out of the club," Melody explained. "North and I went looking for you."

"Where were you, Claire?" Dee Dee asked.

"Just…er…riding around."

"Where?"

"Please…please…don't meddle, Mother," Melody pleaded.

"Meddle?"

"Just don't, Mother—" Melody begged.

When Melody had jilted North, Dee Dee had been devastated. What had snapped her out of her depression had been having him to dinner when Claire was home for spring break. She had advised Claire to be sweet to him and had encouraged their friendship.

"Melody and North were in the living room till two, but I didn't hear you come in last night, dear," Dee Dee persisted. "You know how I worry when you don't come in and kiss me." She skimmed the newspaper headlines. "Oh dear…. Another one of those silly wars…"

"It was late. I didn't want to bother you."

"So, have you talked to North this morning?" Dee Dee demanded, setting her paper down and picking up the stack of bills.

Melody's gaze was strangely *alight*.

"Not yet," Claire said.

Oddly enough, she didn't care that he hadn't called. For no reason at all, Claire forgot Melody and North and her mother. Again she saw *him* standing in the pilothouse of his shrimp boat, barefoot, in nothing but his ragged jeans,

the wheel sliding through his long tanned fingers, his hair
rumpled and dark, his painted mustache and silver gaze
more disturbingly attractive than ever. He'd caught her to
him, placed her between himself and the wheel. She'd
leaned against him and placed the black patch over his eye
again.

He'd laughed, held her close, sheltering her in his arms.
She'd felt so safe, so complete.

Forget him. It was a dream. Only a dream.

Then why did he seem so real?

"Your ring—" Dee Dee said.

"My...my what...?" Claire looked down at her hand.
Where was it?

Then she remembered.

She fumbled for words. "I—I put it in my purse."

"Oh...dear...dear," Melody said. "You took his ring
off. You *were* mad at North."

Claire closed her ringless left hand, thrust it under her
hip to hide it. Then realizing the gesture was suspicious,
pulled it out, held it up, flexed her fingers with an air of
too-studied innocence. "Maybe for a little while."

"As long as you know where it is, dear," said Dee Dee,
relaxing. She glanced at her watch and gathered up her
checkbook.

Melody's curious gaze was fixed on her sister's white
face.

"It's very expensive, dear," Dee Dee said.

"It's a priceless family heirloom. It was North's grandmother's to be exact," Melody murmured. "He told me all
about it...a long time ago, of course...when he slipped
it..."

Dee Dee blanched.

"What did you talk about last night?" Claire asked as
she got up.

"You, of course," Melody said.

Nightgown billowing, Claire went to the fridge and pretended delight in the accumulation of snapshots, newspaper clippings of wedding festivities, and the tattered copy of the present month from Dee Dee's wall calendar.

In every photograph Claire was perfectly dressed and posed while the pictures of Melody were more offbeat. In one, Claire lounged on a towel in a white bikini and matching, see-through cover-up. Everybody had said she was so beautiful that day. Beside her, Melody, who'd had her friends bury her, was covered to her neck in wet sand. Even her honey-gold hair was caked with gooey sand. Everybody had laughed at Melody. Ignoring the glamorous Claire, the boys had heaped more sand on her fun-loving sister.

Claire read Dee Dee's calendar page that listed meetings, lunch, and the supper party tonight. Number three said, Claire. Bridesmaids. Luncheon. Nana. Country Club.

"Oh, my—" Claire gasped and then smiled. "I'd better wash my hair."

"I'll be in my office trying to scrape up enough money to pay for some of these. Hang your pink dress on your doorknob...so Lucia can press it. And don't forget to pick up your black sheath at the cleaners," Dee Dee said.

"Black? I'm not into fashion...but a bride...in black?" Melody asked.

"It has a designer label. It has a lacy collar that's white," Dee Dee retorted. "It was very expensive."

Black's your color, taunted an all-too-familiar, pirate voice in the back of Claire's mind.

Strip, my lady. Slowly.

Claire smiled a little too brightly. "I...I can't wait to wear it."

Oh, how she wished she could undo what she'd done. Oh, how she wished she'd never met the biker. In the past, lots of her friends had bragged to her about impulsive, one-night trysts. Alarmed and amazed, she'd listened to their whispered confessions about men who brought out their wild side.

But they'd all gone on with their lives.

Somehow, she would too.

Strip, my lady. Slowly.

Color crept up behind the high collar of her nightgown. For no reason at all her fingertips began to massage the bruised place on her neck where his lips had marked her.

Her friends hadn't been consumed with guilt and embarrassment. They hadn't hurt their families, thrown their whole lives away.

His name. She didn't even know his name.

Suddenly Claire was running from the kitchen, through the dining room, past the swirling stairs, down the long hall that led to her room on the far side of the house.

"Claire?" Dee Dee stepped out of her office. "Claire!"

Claire stopped. "What—"

"Why don't you borrow some of my concealer for those shadows under your eyes."

And for your neck, teased Loverboy.

"Shut up!"

"What dear?"

"Nothing, Mother."

Safe in her room, Claire fell across her bed and lay staring at her ringless finger as if her blood was sluggish and she lacked the energy to even rise.

Strangely what she wanted far more than North's ring was to know her fantasy pirate's real name.

Seven

Lush red bougainvillea dripped charmingly from the trellis above Claire's patio, adding just the right touch to her feminine bedroom with the antique canopy bed that had belonged to Aunt Sister, the aunt who had raised her mother. The bed had a pink bedspread that matched her overstuffed chairs and their floral slipcovers. Usually her perfect room was a refuge.

Not today.

Wet hair hanging over her face like a mop, wrapped in a towel, Claire was on her hands and knees on her floor. With trembling fingers she shook out her purse and then searched through the empty bag and the contents on her white carpet, her heart racing in panic.

She picked up the shell, the feather, the black satin eye patch. No ring!

Her change purse must have fallen out in his bedroom.

Had he found it?

What would he do when he did?

What could she do?

Dear God.

Then she heard Melody singing in the hall, and her sister's voice was getting louder as she came closer.

Claire couldn't let on how upset she was; somehow she had to act calm and poised.

As fast as lightning, Claire shoved her purse and all its contents under her bed. Then she raced to her vanity and turned her hair-dryer full blast and began blow-drying her hair.

Melody came up close and shouted in her ear.

"So, where is it?"

Claire's skin went hot and clammy.

Melody pointed to her ringless finger. "Your three-carat wonder!"

Claire's heart thudded. "I-I don't want to talk about it."

"I bet you don't want to talk about where you went last night, either."

Claire sucked in a breath.

"North and I waited for you for hours," Melody continued. "Don't get mad. When you didn't come in last night, I covered for you."

"What?"

"Didn't you wonder who stuffed all those pillows under your sheets? I threw some of your clothes and hair rollers all over the place, and shut your door, so she'd think you were asleep if she checked on you this morning as usual."

"Thank you."

"I...I saw how upset you were when you left the party."

Melody's smile was so endearingly warm, it touched a soft place in Claire's heart. There had been a strain between them for too long.

"Oh, Mel— This wedding. It's got me so crazy. You wouldn't believe."

"Oh, yes, I would. Why do you think I ran? All those wedding parties! Having to live up to North's family's expectations…knowing I couldn't…. I was always wearing the wrong dresses, saying the wrong things. Do you remember how furious his grandmother got when I wore tennis shoes under my formal because I'd hurt my foot running? I was just completely overwhelmed. At least…last night…North and I talked it out."

"Why did you come home without telling us?"

"Have you ever done anything impulsive in your whole life?"

Oh, yes.

"I was afraid to call," Melody said. "I guess because I didn't know if you'd want me here."

"Oh, Mel… Mel…"

"I never felt so lonely and weird in my whole life as I did on that freighter to China. All I could think of was you and North getting married. I was afraid to call. I hurt…I hurt so many people. So, I just came home. I felt so guilty…like such a failure…and that just made me madder at all of you. Especially you…the perfect daughter…. Why couldn't I ever be perfect like you?"

"Me? Perfect? Everybody adores *you.*"

"They adore the clown. That's not me. I've always been afraid to play the straight guy, to be serious, to let anybody close enough to really know who I am. Even North. Not that he's important." She hesitated. "Even you. Everybody's proud of you. They respect you."

Respect.

If they only knew.

Strip, my lady.

"I…I can't believe…."

Swiftly they were in each other's arms. Their hug was brief, and afterward they shared a long quiet look.

"Thanks," Claire said. "Thanks for coming home. I—I think we're more alike…than we know."

"I owe you," Melody whispered, her eyes and cheeks aglow in a way they had not been for a very long time. "Maybe more than I can ever repay. I had to come home. I had no choice about that. But I'm sorry…about dancing like that last night. You ran out because of me. I—I felt so unsure of my welcome…. When I feel scared, I act crazy, so people will clap or laugh. Whatever happened, wherever you went, last night was my fault."

"I lost North's ring, Melody," Claire confided.

"Then I'll help you get it back."

Immediately, Claire regretted her confession. "No. No. Forget we had this conversation. Last night's our secret."

Claire looked at the red bougainvillea dripping onto her patio, so she didn't see her sister's gaze go to the mark a certain pirate's mouth had left on her throat.

"You know, Claire, I don't think anybody ever forgets anything. Especially not secrets or mysteries or anything having to do with sex."

"Sex! For goodness sake, Melody. You have the wildest imagination."

At just that moment Melody saw a length of black ribbon under Claire's dust ruffle. She knelt and picked up what turned out to be a black silk eye patch.

"Hmmm?"

Melody's curious gaze rose to her sister's flaming face. When she put the eye patch over one eye, Claire's heart thundered.

Carefully, she hid her panic. "Give me that," she said quietly.

Melody dropped the eye patch in her sister's open palm.

Claire closed her fingers, but just the feel of the warm black silk made her ache.

"Wild imaginations run in this family," Melody said softly. "Sometimes they're our downfall."

The swimming pool was the centerpiece of Dee Dee's flower bejeweled backyard that contained acres of well-manicured lawn and flowerbeds, terraces, a hot tub and a playhouse that was a perfect replica of the larger mansion. Winding gravel drives ran through thick clumps of yellow daisies to the various outhouses.

Still wet from their afternoon swim Claire and Melody, their eyes closed, lay side by side, not speaking, their paperback books face down on matching little wicker tables beside their chaise lounges. Yet, the sisters were very preoccupied with each other.

Even though Claire had to wear a high-collared dress, she'd played the happy bride to perfection at Nana's luncheon. She'd chatted easily with everyone, and had laughed constantly. She'd been so good that she'd fooled everyone, even herself...for a time.

But Melody had played the clown, stolen the show, entertained the crowd. All the old sibling rivalries had been revived. The minute the luncheon was over, Claire had felt completely drained. When she'd come out for a swim, Melody had followed her.

"I guess you and North plan to build a house like this."

Claire didn't want to talk about North to Melody. "Do you remember all the fights Mother and Daddy had over it?"

"Only bigger," Melody persisted, "because North is so much richer than Daddy."

Dee Dee had trained them both from birth that marrying a lowly doctor would never, ever do. Their mother knew this because she'd made that very mistake. In south Texas, a girl with social aspirations had to marry big money or old money. Oil money and the big ranch were the ultimate status symbols. Sam had a habit of digging in his heels when it came to spending the kind of money it took to impress the people Dee Dee wanted to impress.

Which was why Dee Dee thought North was so perfect. He had acres and acres of money, and all those cows and horses and oil wells to sweeten his legendary name.

Melody sighed. "Did you find North's ring?"

Claire's still face gave her away.

"Where *did* you go last night?"

Claire said nothing.

"Why do I feel like I'm playing Twenty Questions?"

That brought a fleeting smile.

"Who put that mark on your throat?"

Claire's hand rushed to her neck. But it was covered. She was wearing a high-collared shirt over her swimsuit. She'd even swum in it. Where, when, how had Melody seen the bruise?

Again Claire felt that damp, salt-laden breeze caressing her. Again, she saw a dark hand tracing her belly with a white feather until she shivered and pulled him on top of her.

"Did he dress up like a pirate?"

"I—I can't talk about it."

"But we have to get North's ring back."

"That's not so easy. Someone...someone I can't possibly see again...has it."

"This someone...in a black eye patch, who kissed you?" Melody's tone brightened. "Why do I imagine this someone tall and dark...and...and gorgeous...male, of course."

"Too male," Claire admitted on a breathy note. "And awful. Except...except he did save my life."

"And you repaid him with a torrid kiss—"

"No!"

"Then he stole it?"

"Don't tease. Not about this."

"Did he steal the ring, too?"

He stole a far more precious jewel, taunted Loverboy.

"What's his name?"

With a cry, Claire buried her face in her hands.

"Could I go get it for you—"

Claire flushed hotly. "Stay away from him."

"Claire, you have to get it back."

"Nobody must know about him. There are reasons, good reasons, why I don't want to see him again."

"I'm sure." Melody chewed on a fingernail which was how she always did her best thinking. "Look, do you remember that awful P.I.? That patient of Daddy's who didn't pay his surgery bill? The guy Daddy hired to find me when I ran out on North?"

"The guy you made walk the plank."

Melody laughed. "Him!"

"Why would he help you?"

"He couldn't swim, and I threw him a life raft. He's like a bloodhound. He'll get your ring back. When you have it on your finger again, you can relax and go on with your life."

Which was exactly what Claire wanted to do. "Why are you helping me?"

"You're my sister."

"What about North?"

"We worked out our differences last night. But our romance and North's love for me ended a long time ago." Melody fell silent. "I—I can tell you're upset about the ring...and about what happened last night, that's all," she whispered, her gaze drifting to her sister's high, white collar. "Some kiss, huh?"

Claire shuddered. Instead of the ring, she thought of a man who was tall and dark and slim, yet powerfully built. A man in a pirate costume with a jeering white smile, a man who'd slung her over his wide shoulder and carried her to bed. She thought of all the bold kisses he'd given her as well as the other intimacies they'd shared.

"I'm not nearly as upset about the ring as...as I am about him," she breathed, little chills darting up her arms. "That's why I—I can't hire your P.I. to go over there. I—I don't even know his name."

"Do you know where *he* lives?"

Claire rubbed her arms. "Rockport. Not far from our condo." Nervously she answered a few of Melody's questions and then stopped, immediately wishing she'd never discussed this with her unpredictable sister. "Melody, it's very important you don't do something rash. I have to be very, very careful. He's got a temper...and...and powerful feelings. If he finds out who I am...or where I live...if I make him angry...I... I...don't know what he might do."

Just thinking about him stripped her soul bare of all but a single truth.

A truth she did not want to see.

Melody's eyes measured her, and a dangerous flutter of emotion danced inside Claire.

Claire jumped up, grabbed her towel. "Forget what I told you, Melody. Just forget it. Forget him."

Melody rose and very gently flipped her sister's collar down. "What if I can't?" She studied the bruise. "What if you can't forget the man who kissed you like that?"

"Whatever you do, don't hire that P.I."

"At least then...you'd know *his* name."

Eight

The sleaze with the crowbar hacking at Tag's back door was a bowlegged runt on the wrong side of forty.

"That son-of-a...a..." Because of the thin, black boy beside him, Tag bit back a string of curses.

"Son-of-a-dachshund," Ricky Navarro, Tag's young friend, supplied with a mischievous grin. Ricky was eleven and atremble with excitement.

Too furious to smile back, Tag hugged Ricky reassuringly just as Whiskers plopped in the grass at his feet. Next Trousers, Tag's Border collie slunk by, his tail between his legs.

"Some watchdog you are," Tag muttered.

"He only barks at friends," said Ricky.

Several of his other stray cats and dogs moved through the grass with equal stealth. The group watched the incompetent intruder.

Crooks came in all shapes and sizes. This one working

on Tag's door had thinning hair and wire-rimmed glasses. He had a florid complexion and a spare tire around the middle section of his slight frame. He wore a black Stetson and black silver-tipped boots that matched his jeans. He was huffing hard and drenched in sweat. The guy was in lousy shape.

Tag's eyes glittered. His fingers tightened on the boy's shoulder.

This was about her.

For the past few nights he'd lain in bed dreaming about her coming back and the games he'd make her play before he gave her back the ring.

She'd had her fill of him, so she'd sent a hired hand to do her dirty work.

Tag hunkered beside Ricky in the high grass at the edge of the wood.

"Told you it wasn't a woman, huh?" Ricky's black eyes shone with their usual hero worship.

"You did good. Real good."

He'd been repairing a net on the dock when Ricky's skinny black legs had come pounding down the dock, shouting that there was a man breaking into his house.

"You gonna buy me another Millennium 2000?" Ricky whispered, black eyes aglow.

A Millennium 2000 was long for yo-yo.

"If it doesn't set me back more than twenty bucks."

"It won't!"

The boy began to fidget in the high brown grass near the twisted oaks with acute discomfort. "Hey, there's stickers."

"You should've worn shoes."

Wood splintered. The door fell off its hinges with a crash, bouncing down the steps. Then the bastard was inside.

"Ricky, you stay put."

"But I wanna see you kick some dachshund butt."

"Your Mama says you aren't supposed to talk like that."

"She talks like that every time she watches the Cowboys play and the other team makes a touchdown."

"What women tell us we should do and what they do themselves is different."

Tag crawled toward his house.

"What are you gonna do without your gun?" Ricky whispered.

"Shhh."

"Just in case he whups you or finds your gun before you do, I stuck an icepick in his front tire, so he won't drive off real fast the way that blonde did. She sure was pretty. Prettier than all the others…"

"You been spying on my house?"

"She had a shell and a feather. She kissed them. She was crying when she got in her car."

Tag hated the way his heart hurt.

"You gonna marry her—"

"I said shhh."

Stray cats scattered as Tag scrambled on his knees down the length of his breezeway. Curses and dishes exploded from the kitchen. As Tag raced down the hall, he noted that his usually tidy house was a shambles. Sofa, tables, chairs—everything had been turned over.

In the kitchen the man was bent over. Breathing hard, he slid an open palm across the dark insides of a cabinet. A single lunge from the doorway and Tag and the man were sprawled on the floor. Tag yanked his hair, got him by the throat. The son-of-a-dachshund's bulging eyes darted wildly. His arms flayed helplessly.

"What'd ya bet a pretty girl from Corpus Christi sent you?"

Their eyes clashed. When the man didn't answer, Tag dug in his back pocket and yanked out a wallet.

"Merle Mello. P.I." Tag snorted. "What's her name?"

When he didn't answer, Tag shook him. Then he leaned down and spoke very softly against his ear. "I want her name, Merle."

"You give me the ring you stole, and I'll give you the money she paid me."

"I'm not for sale, you lousy bastard. I'll give her ring back—but on my terms."

"Which are?" The man's voice held a tinge of nervousness.

"First, her name."

"I ain't ever gonna tell."

Tag laughed. "You wanna bet?"

A tangerine sky and a reddening sea bathed Claire in a pink glow. In her white shorts, with her hair swept away from her face in a headband, she made a pretty picture on her daddy's yacht, *Fanta-Sea,* as she scrubbed a stanchion. Claire had decided it was time, way past time to make up with North. Since *that* night, they'd talked once. He was busy at the ranch, he said, working some nights till midnight, trying to get ahead before their wedding. She'd said she'd let him work, that she would concentrate on the wedding. Their brief conversation had been cool and strangely stilted as if each of them were holding something back.

Tonight she was going to change all that.

The preacher was coming over to talk about the ceremony tonight. North was supposed to have called to find out what time an hour ago. So, why hadn't he?

Claire wasn't concentrating on her handiwork nearly as hard as she was polishing. She was too aware of seconds ticking by, of the orange light behind the skyline deepening and darkening. Too aware that she really didn't care if North ever called. These last few days with him out of the picture hadn't bothered her nearly as much as they should have. What bothered her were memories of a man she had to forget.

It was a funny thing about the people who owned yachts. They might have maids for such menial chores at home, but they performed these same tasks on their boats themselves. Sam Woods, who wouldn't even reach down to put a dirty sock in his hamper, loved cleaning his boat. When he wasn't onboard polishing teak or chrome, he could usually talk his wife or a daughter into doing it.

She had used polishing as an excuse to get away from the house, away from all the perfection and pretense of her life. She needed to prepare for the preacher and North, time to think more positively about her future.

Strangely, the salt-laden air and the lapping of the water made her remember those same sights and sounds from the night she'd spent with the biker. She still didn't have a clue as to how she could get her ring back. Melody kept begging her to let her hire that detective, but she kept telling her no.

When her cell phone finally buzzed, Claire dropped the toothbrush and dug frantically in her purse for her phone.

"North?" she breathed. With an effort she put more excitement in her tone. "Darling, I thought you'd never call—"

"Hello, Claire." The hard voice shook her to the core. Her feet felt leaden. Her heart raced. She sank to her knees, pressed the phone against her ear.

Dear God—

When she could breathe, she whispered, "Who…who is this?"

But she knew.

"You little liar. You know damn well who—" His voice was deeper, gruffer. "Captain *X.*"

The name and the memories that went with it sent a shiver through her.

"But maybe it's time you had a real name to go with the motorcycle and the pirate costume…and your fantasy lover, Captain *X*. It's Tag Campbell."

Tag Campbell.

Just his name stung her heart.

Oh, God, he'd found her.

She began to tremble.

"I have something you want," he purred. "Something valuable."

"Oh, yes…. Yes, you do." Her words were barely audible.

"What price are you willing to pay…to get it back?"

He sounded so cruel, so changed.

"I…I'm through playing games."

"You shouldn't have started this one then, pretty lady."

Why was he so angry? "No—"

"Yes!" he rasped. "Think of this as a simple business proposition. I have something you want. You have something I want. You give me what I want. I give you what you want. It's real simple—sweetheart."

"But I don't know what you want!"

In the lengthening silence she began to shiver.

His deep, dark voice bit. "Was I so easy to forget?"

His question brought tumult. Guilt crept over her. Pain seared her.

No way could she tell him that every night she'd lain in bed for hours, unable to sleep, remembering how scared she'd been, remembering he'd saved her from those thugs and been so sweet afterwards. No way could she admit that all her dreams were of him now.

"You were very easy to forget," she said.

"Maybe it's time I made more of an impression," he muttered thickly.

Seething sexual tension charged the silence. Before she could reply, he hung up.

She sucked in huge gulps of air.

The phone rang again.

"He-hello," she stammered, her voice strange and hollow and yet...and yet eager, too.

"You sound excited," North said matter-of-factly. "Sorry I'm so late calling you. What time do you want me to come tonight?"

Nine

Tag picked up his straight razor and then threw it into the lavatory. He was going to Corpus—to see her.

The thought both angered and excited him. Just as her soft voice had angered and excited him when she'd called him darling, thinking he was her fiancé.

She'd slept with him, but she called another man darling.

Tag strode into his bathroom and turned on the shower. Then he caught a glimpse of his dark, unshaven reflection in the mirror and frowned. His black shirt was dirty. So were his jeans. He'd worked hard on the boat for nearly twenty-four hours, driven his captains hard, too. He'd worked long hours in the restaurant. Much of his drive came from an effort to quit thinking about her. It hadn't succeeded. Nothing had. Still, the catches had been good. His captains had done well, too. Business at the restaurant had never been better.

Money. He'd always been good at making money. Too good.

"It's your gift," Frenchy had said.

A gift that had nearly destroyed him once.

"You're like a money machine," his father had said.

His father had used him, ruined him, despised him—betrayed him.

You're damn sure no son of mine

I didn't do it. Hugh couldn't have. You did. Nobody knows as much about the business as you.

Except you.

You're not taking me down.

You were born in the gutter.

Whose fault is that?

You've got her bad blood.

Yours, too.

Salt crusted his skin and black hair. He stank of sweat, saltwater, and dead sea things. He craved a shower, clean clothes, a hot meal. No, he craved her and despised himself for the hunger.

He turned off the shower.

For any other woman he would've showered and primped.

Not for her.

Not tonight.

And he'd smell worse by the time he got to Corpus.

He could almost feel the warm clean water splashing his skin, soothing his nerves; almost feel freshly pressed denim.

Not for her.

His life had been hellish ever since she'd left.

For himself he washed his face and brushed his teeth. But that was all. When Trousers barked and bounded into the bathroom, soft brown eyes aglow with love, tail thumping against his leg, Tag knelt and embraced his wet dog, knowing full well the dog smell would cling. Let it.

Since she'd shared his bed, Claire Woods had rarely been

off his mind. He remembered her taste, the silkiness of her hair, the sleek texture of her skin as he'd entered her.

You were very easy to forget, she'd whispered in that sexy, scared tone that tore his heart out.

When he finished roughing Trousers's ears, he didn't bother to comb his own hair. Halfway out the back door, he stopped, then stomped back inside, opened a cabinet and grabbed a bottle of cheap gin. This he splashed all over his grimy T-shirt. Then he hopped on his bike and gunned it.

"We're playin' by my rules tonight, pretty lady."

An hour later he was in Corpus Christi. The evening sea breezes were cooler against Tag's sunburned face as he braked his big bike in sun-dappled shade. From there, he studied the numbers on the houses.

Her tall white mansion was like a punch in the gut. The white pillars reminded him of his father's home, of his own former life. Like his father's, this mansion could have been in a photograph in one of those glossy home and garden magazines. Her street was a wide, tree-lined avenue with large houses built to impress and set back on spacious lawns.

A young red-haired mother pushing a stroller with a plump toddler glanced his way. Ducking her head, the woman hurriedly changed sides of the street and raced away from him.

Lady, you didn't even get close enough to get a whiff.

Suddenly he regretted the gin and not showering and changing. What was he trying to prove? He felt as ashamed as when he was a kid and the son of the town's drunken cocktail waitress who slept around. People used to avoid his mother and him. The kids at school had despised him, never seeing him as human.

Then his father had taught him how to dress, taught him what it took to make people admire him. And for what?

Frenchy and the other shrimpers he knew were a rough

bunch. They didn't care much about following other people's rules. Tag had been hiding in their midst so long he'd nearly forgotten who he was. But this house and this street and this woman made him remember who he'd been and all that he'd wanted.

He studied her front door so long that his throat closed up. Then he swallowed against the dryness, removed his helmet, and swung a long leg over the leather seat.

Maybe he would've lost his nerve, but her front door swung open. A woman with a beautiful smile and thick masses of straight, honey-colored hair held out her hand to him.

Not Claire. Not as pretty as Claire. But nice in her own sparkly way.

When he clasped her hand, she puckered her nose the way a kitten sniffs the air. "Dog," she murmured. "And?"

He smiled. "Gin."

"Shrimp, too." She pinched her nose and then laughed, looking him over. "My. My. You and my sister?"

"Is Claire here?"

"She's around…somewhere. I'm Melody."

Instantly charmed, he smiled. "Tag Campbell. I should've showered—"

"But you're like me—impulsive. Not like Claire—who isn't."

"People can fool you."

Again, she smiled. "So you met my sister that night when she was driving around—"

"Is that what she said?"

Again Melody smiled. "She hasn't been too talkative lately."

"Stress," he whispered. "Brides are under lots of stress."

"Especially brides that don't want to be brides. How well I know." Her smile grew warier when she led him into the foyer. "You be quiet now, and we'll try to find Claire without stirring the rest of the pack up."

"Thanks."

Except for the voluptuous wallpaper, the mansion was amazingly like his father's on the inside. There were the same gleaming oak floors, the usual antiques, the glittering silver-framed photographs of family and celebrities on the grand piano, the same crystal rose bowls with their warmly glowing candles.

The wallpaper was really something, though. Lush, boldly colored flowers seemed to grow out of every wall, to race across the high ceilings above him so that he almost felt he'd stepped into an exotic garden.

From some nearby room he heard the clink of silver and china as well as subdued voices.

Where was Claire?

Melody attempted to lead him swiftly by the partially closed doors of the formal dining room, but a woman's sharp, curious voice stopped them.

"Darling... Melody?" The shrill voice went higher. "What's that smell?"

"He's come to see Claire."

The woman got up. She was beautiful, golden, thin. Like her daughters.

"I thought North—" The blond woman pushed the doors further apart. She wrinkled her elegant nose in disgust. "What is that awful smell?"

"Me," Tag said.

"Gin," the older woman corrected.

"You do know your liquor," he said.

"Cheap gin," she declared.

A plump man in wire-rimmed glasses and a clerical collar stared in outrage.

The rumpled bear with a thatch of silver hair slouching in his chair, turned. He knew trouble when he saw it. One look at Tag, and he bolted his red wine. "And just how would you know our Claire?" Claire's father demanded.

"She had car trouble. I helped her."

"Then why hasn't she once mentioned you?" the mother demanded, her tone shrill.

"Because she had too good a time and she's no dummy," Melody suggested, slinging gasoline onto the flames.

Whoof!

Mr. Woods shoved his chair back from the table. "I've told her and told her not to ride around in that car at night. That she could meet the wrong sort—"

"Let me handle this," his wife commanded.

Mr. Woods poured himself more wine. "You must've scared some sense into her. She's sure been underfoot a lot more. She won't even go out with North."

"Maybe we shouldn't speculate," said Melody. "Maybe we should go straight to the source."

Tag heard light, nervous footsteps and pivoted.

Claire.

Tag sucked in a breath when he saw her. So did she.

Silence.

Breathless, her cheeks pink, a tiny pulse pounding in her throat, she was incredibly sexy in tight jeans and a snug, white T-shirt that molded her slim curves. She looked clean and lovely and fresh as he was foul and stale. So lovely, his anger lessened, and he wished he'd showered and changed for her. All he wanted to do was wrap his arms around her.

"I've been working on the boat with my men," he said as an excuse.

Her huge, blue eyes fastened on his face and didn't let go. She went paper-white, took a step back, faltered and stood still.

"Where's North?" demanded her father.

Silence.

"I thought North was coming," her mother pressed.

Claire's cheeks flamed. "He is."

"Well, this…this man is here to see you."

"He won't be long." Claire's tone was clear and cool, and so dismissive it made Tag's stomach knot. And yet her eyes and the bright fire in her face made him burn.

"Can I fix you a drink?" Melody offered, her sympathetic voice so light it cut the tension. "Gin your special poison?"

"Scotch and water," Tag said.

"Claire?"

"Nothing. Thank you."

Ice cubes clinked. Melody handed him the drink, and Claire quickly said, "Let's go out back…to the pool."

He smiled. "I could use a swim."

Her lips barely moved. "Don't make this harder."

She turned abruptly and fled across the living room, about to slip through a pair of tall, double doors. Beyond those doors stretched a vast expense of greenery, terraces and a swimming pool.

He raced to catch her at the door. Holding it open, he bowed low, as he had the night he'd made love to her.

"Please…." she begged.

He downed his drink and might have set it on an antique table had not Dee Dee, who was right behind him, said, "I'll take that."

"Thank you, Mother," Claire said.

"Claire?!? Don't be a fool. Are you really going out there—alone? With him?"

He turned to catch the mother mouthing frantic entreaties to Claire who was waving goodbye by fluttering her fingertips.

"I'll be fine, Mother," Claire said. "He won't hurt me."

Tag shut the door, and after another long exchange of

glances and fingertip fluttering between mother and daughter, the older woman marched off in a huff.

"Alone at last," he whispered.

"You stink like a brewery."

"Gin," he corrected. "Among other things."

"Did you drive your motorcycle all the way from Rockport drunk?"

"Would you give a damn?"

"Answer my question first." Underneath her anger, she was pleading with him somehow.

"I haven't had a drink for days. Not till the one Melody just gave me. I've been working too hard. Falling into bed every night with a book. Not that I can concentrate on what I read. I pass out with exhaustion, the book still open on my chest." He didn't say he'd done all these things in a futile attempt to forget a woman with long golden hair who reminded him of an angel riding the wind.

In the quiet evening afterglow, Claire was as incandescent and fragile and lovely as the most exquisite white orchid. She smelled sweet, too.

"It's your turn," he whispered, moving closer.

"What?" Instinctively she backed away from him into the shadows.

"Would you give a damn if I drove drunk?"

"Naturally, I wouldn't want you to hit an innocent person...."

"But you don't care what happens to me?"

He let his gaze drop from her pale face—to her mouth, her neck, her breasts—then for good measure, he reversed the order.

"You look good, Claire."

She wet her dry lips.

"Too good."

A hot dangerous spark lit the air between them.

"Do you have the ring?" she whispered.

"You don't care?" he repeated in a hoarse voice. "That's why you want this exchange to be quick and easy?"

"Why torture ourselves—"

"Is that what we're doing?"

"You don't fit into my life. I told you that."

"What if I was different?"

"You're even wilder than you were the first night."

A primal awareness fluttered between them.

"You liked me that night," he reminded her.

Her voice was softer, hesitant. "You're a shrimper. I'm going to be a doctor."

"Do you give people labels? Is that the only way you can think? I've been other things besides a shrimper. I could be more." His voice was darker, deeper. "I'm a man and you're a woman."

"Don't—"

His lips scarcely moved. "You think you're so superior to me. You sent that man to tear up my house, like I'm nothing, like my house is nothing—"

"I don't know what you're talking about."

"Merle. The P.I. you hired."

"But I didn't—"

"You didn't give a damn what he did as long as you got what you wanted. You wanted to play pirate. You wanted sex. Now you want to forget me. You want your ring back. You're used to getting what you want effortlessly."

"Not…not everything."

"Name one thing you want and don't have."

She stared at his mouth. Then she touched her own lips with her fingers. "Please…please just give me the ring and go."

"Maybe I've missed you. Maybe I'm curious as to how you've really been, too."

"I told you I'm fine."

"You don't look fine. You look upset. Scared."

She whirled angrily. "Because you're here."

"You don't really want to marry him."

"I do."

"How come you slept with me when you're engaged to him?"

"I...I wasn't myself. That...that bump on the head... those guys.... I was so scared.... Temporary insanity."

"You were a virgin. You'd never slept with him. Don't tell me you couldn't have if you'd wanted to."

"North isn't like you. He never pushes himself on me sexually."

"That's mighty suspicious behavior."

"To a man...with...with your low instincts maybe."

"The girl who wanted to play games with a pirate has no low instincts?" he mocked.

Her face burned. Her voice shook. "North would never come over here...filthy...to deliberately humiliate me."

"You wanted me."

"This is all Melody's fault."

"Charming girl. At least I know who to thank."

"She danced for North the night I met you. She used to be in love with him, you see, engaged even. I didn't like the way he watched her. I ran out because I was...jealous. When I met you, after those guys in the alley, I didn't know what I was doing."

"This isn't about Melody. You knew exactly what you were doing. You wanted me. You still do."

"I want my ring."

"You can have it." He paused. "But for a price."

"W-what...what do you want?"

"A kiss."

"That's insane." But her soft, slightly breathy gasp warmed him.

He smiled. "I know."

"One kiss?"

He nodded.

"Just one?" She drew another quick breath. "And you'll give me the ring?"

A smile brushed his mouth. "That's what I said."

"Okay," she said quickly, closing her eyes, tilting her chin up to his, and puckering her lips.

He was tempted, mighty tempted by her beauty, by her sweet, soft scent, most of all by her lips. But unlike her, he wanted to prolong the moment.

When all he did was brush her hair back from her face, she jumped, her eyes snapping open.

"Uh-uh." He grinned down at her. "You have to kiss me."

"I can't believe you're making me do this."

"Believe it."

She reached up, and he felt her lips peck the side of his throat, just under his left ear. A single flutter of breath and fire, and it was over.

"On my lips," he ordered.

"You didn't say—"

"That's what I meant."

Even before she did it, he felt his blood race like a heat wave and his heart pound like he'd been running hard. Only he hadn't moved. Once she settled her mouth on his, once she started, he wasn't about to let her stop.

Cautiously her lips settled on his, and he felt a rush of pure, sweet sensation. His chest tightened. He opened his mouth, answered her kiss. And was stunned she let him.

When he wrapped her in his arms, she clung, shuddering.

After all the lonely days and nights, holding her was heaven. She closed her eyes. Kissing her was ecstasy.

"I want more than one kiss," he whispered, his eyes burning into hers. "You know that, don't you?"

She swallowed, but she didn't pull away. Instead she pressed herself against him, put her arms around his neck, caressed his face with her light fingertips. Then her mouth found his again.

The second kiss was sweeter and lasted longer and told him how much she'd missed him. He caressed her face, and the longing that cut through him cut through her, too. They began to shake.

"You have the softest lips, and the hardest body," she murmured.

"Claire, is everything all right?"

Her mother's voice cracked them like a whip.

Claire stiffened, pushed him angrily away. "You got what you wanted," she whispered. "So, give me the ring." Then in a louder voice, she called to her mother. "Yes…everything's all right, Mother."

"North's here."

"I'll just be a minute, Mother."

When Tag tried to pull Claire back into his arms, she drew a quivering breath before pushing him away. "He's here. You've got to give me the ring and go."

"You don't love him."

"I will. I swear I will."

"But you don't now. And you never will. And deep down you're afraid I'm right."

Impulsively, she feathered protesting fingertips against his lips. Just as impulsively, he began to kiss those fingers.

"Please…. I'm begging you."

"The road to hell is paved with good intentions," he said, a desperate tone tinging his voice. "I can't get you out of my mind. I thought I'd die if I didn't see you again. Only now that I've seen you, I feel even worse."

"So do I. I'm marrying North Black. I want my ring. If I'd met you under different circumstances…but I didn't. If you were different…"

If he wasn't a low, filthy shrimper.

"All right. You win." He yanked the ring out of his pocket, but instead of giving it to her, he knelt before her like a besotted suitor.

"Hand it to me!"

"And I thought you were a romantic." He took her hand in his, and the minute he stroked her fingers, felt how they shook, some of the anger left him. He pressed his lips against her fingers, held on to them tightly when she tried to tug them away.

"Do hurry," she whispered.

"Did North hurry that night?" he rasped. "Or did he get on his knees like this when he proposed?"

"Don't—"

On his knees, in an attitude of lover-like worship, Tag pressed her hand to his lips again. Only this time he kissed each finger, sliding his warm tongue between them, causing her to shiver.

"Don't you dare do that again!"

"Did he dare? Do you drive him wild the way you do me?" His low voice was savaged by emotion. "Claire, I can't forget you. No matter how I try. I lie awake and think I can't live without you beside me in that bed. I've never felt so alone. I'll quit shrimping. I wasn't always a shrimper. I can be what you want. I can make money. Lots of money. It's easy for me. There's nothing, Claire, nothing I wouldn't do for you or give you. Did he say these things to you?"

Claire was ill-prepared to deal with the ferocity of his mock proposal, and the passion in his voice brought a sigh to her lips, for North had proposed in a brightly-lit restaurant. He'd been on the run because he had to get back to the ranch. In separate cars, she'd driven back to school, and he'd driven back to his ranch.

"Just give me the ring," she said, refusing to dwell on the disappointment of North's proposal.

Tag slid the ring over her knuckle ever so carefully. "You have beautiful hands. Did he tell you that?"

"Be quiet about North, do you understand?"

"Don't marry him."

"I have to."

"The night I met you, I was at the cemetery. I'd just buried my best friend."

"I'm sorry."

"I hadn't known what a friend he was till... I was scared. God, I was scared. Then you were there. Like a magical being, lighting something inside me that had been dead for years. A comfort in a dark hour."

She ran a finger lightly over his eyebrow, down his rough cheek, over his smooth high cheekbone. "I'm sorry about your friend." Her voice died away. "Most of all I'm sorry about—"

"Claire, are you still out there?" Her mother's voice slicing the darkness again.

"Coming—"

"Be happy," Tag said.

He didn't know if she heard him because she was already running away, past her mother, into the house.

"Show him out the back way," the mother snapped out coldly to a silent figure behind her. The door slammed, and he felt diminished.

Again, he was that lost little boy outside his father's house in the dark.

Ten

Melody glided toward him through silvery light and gray shadow. "Let's go, Tag."

Numbly, he felt her take his arm as she led him around to the back gate.

Back gates were for servants and other undesirables.

For little boys not worth keeping.

For smelly shrimpers in rough, work clothes. But long before they reached that gate, a liquid movement in a ground-floor bedroom jolted Tag out of his self-pitying mood.

Hair flying behind her like a golden banner, a slim girl ran inside.

Claire. His angel riding the wind.

She flung a wild, lost look around the room and then hurled herself onto her bed. There she buried her head in a wadded pillow and lay still. Her phone rang, but she ignored it. Her fluffy white cat bounded up to her patio door, stretched full length, and began pawing the glass.

"That Claire's bedroom?"

"I shouldn't tell a man like you a thing like that." But her smile said yes.

They stood in the shadows together and watched Claire's slender shoulders heave and her fingers claw her bedspread.

"She's been like that…since the night she met you."

"Hasn't she been with *him?*"

"North? Not once. Tonight's the first time. He's in with Mother and Daddy and the preacher. Nobody but you and me know what's really going on."

"And what's that?"

"Claire and I… We're all mixed up. We've got to get straight."

Melody pointed toward another square of light that was partially obscured by lush climbing roses. Like players, the three figures framed in that glowing cubicle kept mouthing cues, looking toward the door, waiting for the lead actress to come on stage.

"Why don't you go in there and keep that bunch entertained for a spell?"

"You mean you want me to run interference for you?"

Somehow he knew Melody was on his side. "Maybe it's me, who's running interference for you. How come you came back and danced for your sister's man?"

"Sometimes a girl's a fool and she throws away the only thing she really wants."

"The trait must run in the family."

She smiled. "What makes you think you're what my sister wants?"

He pulled Melody close and whispered something into her ear.

She grinned. "I'll do it. It's so dumb it just might work. I'm a little jealous I didn't think of it."

She vanished into the house.

Claire. He was a fool to stay, a fool to scheme. But he couldn't stop watching the way light sparked from the fall of butter-gold hair that hid Claire's features. He ached from watching her slender body quiver on every sob.

This beautiful, special girl had gone to bed with him. He'd been her first man. But she'd been first with him in other ways. She'd pulled feelings out of him, thoughts too, along with secrets that had been festering inside him way too long. He'd been in hiding—from the world, from himself. Frenchy had tried to tell him, but he hadn't cared enough to do anything about it. Not till her.

Like an angel riding the wind, she led him out of his dark cave and set him free. She'd given him comfort, shown him what it was to have feelings for a woman that were good and clean instead of shameful.

He stood in the dark and watched her cat paw the glass. Claire never looked up.

What was that black ribbon she was holding, kissing?

When Melody pranced into the dining room, her mother's face flashed with annoyance. Worse, the tall, tanned rancher turned to stone.

His and Claire's lives weren't the only knots in this tangle.

Tag stepped toward her cat and let it sniff his boot. Then he picked the curious animal up and rapped on her door.

Claire looked up. With glistening eyes she stared straight into his heart.

Chemistry. Neither of them could stop staring once they started.

The cat meowed and began to lick. He felt like a fool in his dirty clothes, holding her sissy cat. Hell, her fiancé was here with the preacher.

But she stepped toward him. As if in a dream, she opened the doors, and took the fluffy, purring bundle of fur clinging to his awful shirt. Her cat had a flat, white face, pale blue eyes and a snaggle tooth that made it charmingly ridiculous.

"She likes you," Claire whispered.

"And she's no mongrel…like my pets."

"But they have pure, gentle hearts."

"Indeed." He paused. "Did it ever occur to you…maybe I do, too?"

"Yes." Her hoarse whisper sounded torn.

She collapsed against his filthy shirt, and he folded her nearer. "Don't cry, baby." Holding her so that her head was tucked under his chin, he sank with her to his knees. "I can't go. Not till you stop crying," he soothed.

"I have to marry him. It's what girls like me are supposed to do."

"Says who?" His voice was soft, almost fatherly.

"You don't know my family. What they expect—" In a few choked words she sobbed out the whole story, about Melody jilting North at the altar, about her mother's smashed hopes and social ambitions, about having to be the perfect daughter to make up for the son who'd died before she was born.

"I don't care what your reasons are. You can't build a life on a lie. I know. I tried."

"I have to make my family happy. You and me—we just met."

He stroked her hair out of her face. "We started something that's bigger than both of us."

"We'll get over it."

His hand froze on her cheek. "How?" The ache in his heart made it hard to breathe. "Are you so young that you really believe that? Do you really think you can make yourself have feelings you don't have?"

"Yes. Mother says—"

"You're a woman now, Claire. You may be young, but it's time you made your own choices. You can't make anybody happy if you don't do that, least of all yourself. Come away with me. We'll go somewhere. For coffee maybe. Just to talk."

"I have a date with North."

"Your first—since me."

"I've…been too busy."

"Or preoccupied with dreams of me." He opened her hand, and his eye patch fluttered to the floor.

She flushed guiltily.

"We are good together," he said. "It wasn't just a game. That's why you don't want to see him."

"I couldn't sleep with you…and then…just start up with him like nothing happened."

"That's reassuring."

"I'm serious."

"So am I."

"He's my fiancé."

Tag scowled.

"Tonight, I really need to talk to him—to try to get to where we were before—"

"Before *us.*"

"There is no us."

"Make it an early date, and come out with me."

"No. This…" She caught her breath. "This, *us,* whatever it is, has to end."

"What if we can't end it?"

"We can."

"If it's so easy, then prove it. Prove it yourself."

"How?"

"I'm going home. Come to me there."

"Alone?"

"Then meet me at Shorty's."

"Shorty's?"

"You remember that bar that played the music we danced to? If you don't show, I'll be drinking to your future

happiness. To your wedded bliss. If you come, if you can
dance one dance, maybe play a game of pool, have some
fun with me…and then walk away…then I'd know for sure
you don't want me.''

''I could do it.''

''Prove it.''

''I have a date.''

The thought of her with another man filled him with
panic. So Tag blurted what he had to say, quick and fast.
''That didn't stop you before.''

''I'm not like you think.''

''Neither am I.''

Claire's eyes widened as the flat countryside swept past
in a frightening blur. Her fingernails dug into her armrest.
Not that she dared ask North to slow down.

He was in one of his moods, his dark hands fisted around
the steering wheel. He hadn't said one word about her tight,
red dress. She might as well be invisible. He hadn't once
looked at her.

What had she expected?

Claire watched the speedometer needle inch upward.
North was a careful man who rarely speeded.

She shot him another worried glance. Beneath the brim
of his Stetson, his dark face was deathly still. He was driving fast, as if something was eating him up on the inside.

''Did the preacher say something that bothered you?''
Claire whispered in a demure tone that did not match her
dress.

''It isn't *him*.''

''But something's bothering you?''

''I'm a little tired.''

''You're scaring me.''

He lifted his foot off the gas. ''What do you feel like
doing tonight? How about a movie?''

They usually went to movies when North got like this. She suspected he preferred sitting in the dark, not talking, to a more intimate date.

"I'm not exactly dressed for a movie," she said a little flirtatiously.

A muscle tensed in his hard jawline. He did look at her then. If he were pleased at all the effort she'd gone to to make herself beautiful for him, he didn't show it. His eyes flared wildly with the look of a wild creature caught in a trap.

"Let's go to Rockport," she urged too gaily. "I—I need to pick up something at the condo for Mother." Just the thought of Rockport got her a little breathless.

"Fine," he said. "Whatever you want, Claire."

He lapsed into a heavy silence that made her increasingly uneasy as flying center stripes vanished too rapidly beneath the car. His grim silence was unnerving her. Did he suspect? The fingers she pressed against her window shook. She flipped on the radio and hummed along to the tunes the way Melody sometimes did.

North pushed a button and turned the radio off. "Don't hum!"

North barely said five words at the condo, but one of them was yes when she asked if he'd take her to Shorty's.

They braked in Shorty's garishly lit, crowded parking lot. When she opened her own door and jumped out, a rough-looking bunch of bikers whistled.

"That dress…" North blurted.

"You finally noticed."

He stared.

The offshore breeze ruffled her hair. This same, prevailing breeze had made all those leaning sculptures out of live oak trees around *his* beach house.

The breeze's salty caress brought memories of a man she couldn't forget.

Music thrummed in the parking lot, the same sort of music they'd danced to outside the beach house.

She was here to prove to *him* she could forget him.

She tossed her head defiantly. The wind rippled through her hair and made her feel wilder.

"You sure about this place?" North asked.

"Very sure," she said. "I've heard the band is good."

"How exactly did you hear that, Claire?"

Without answering, she flung the door open and stepped inside to howls and more whistles.

"You got a date tonight, honey," a soft, silky voice purred behind Tag's ear.

He turned and through a blur of smoke, he saw yellow hair and a shapely figure in a tight red dress. For a second or two his heart raced, just till he realized she wasn't Claire.

God, just thinking *she* might show tonight had him wired.

"I'm waiting for a particular lady." His fingers moved up and down the icy beer bottle.

"Do I know you?" she whispered.

She should, but she didn't.

His silver eyes glazed. "Not really," he replied.

"Your face. Your body. You seem familiar."

He stared past her toward the door.

When she went back to the bar, Tag slouched lower in his shadowy corner table. He'd showered, changed. Dressed in jeans and a black shirt.

A dull pain had settled in his gut. The thought of Claire coming here, to this place, to him, to prove anything, was pretty far-fetched. The girl who'd wept in his arms wasn't about to risk awakening that shadow-sister inside herself again—the one who craved him for her midnight pirate fantasy.

Maybe he was better off. If he'd unleashed her, she'd

done the same for him. Since he was a kid, he'd always wanted a better life, a real family. But every time he'd reached for the stars, doors had slammed shut.

The dimly-lit, crowded bar throbbed with music, women, voices, smoke, and laughter. Men slouched over pool cues and green tables and sent balls clicking and flying.

Except for the blonde, people were mostly leaving him alone. They weren't as angry as they'd been right after Frenchy's death about Frenchy leaving him everything. Rusty and Hank had disappeared. Most people believed the coroner. Some were even beginning to admire the way he'd gotten a tight handle on Frenchy's empire so quickly. He had plans to expand, create jobs and pay solid wages.

The door opened.

The shrimpers at the bar kicked and stomped in time to the music. Wolf whistles. Shouts. Applause.

Tag's gaze jerked back to the door.

Claire, standing in a pink pool of neon light, her pale face frozen in the garish glare as it had been that first night. The music speeded up. Everything and everybody blurred but her.

She wore a tight red dress and her hair fell wildly about her shoulders.

No bright angel tonight.

Tonight her shadow-self had come alive. The gorgeous woman in red pulsed with a wild, dark energy that turned his blood to lava.

When she saw him, she flicked her tongue wetly across her lips and locked her blue gaze on his mouth.

More wolf whistles.

What the hell was she trying to do?

In that dress, with her body, she was setting more fires than she or he could ever put out.

Somebody put a few quarters in the jukebox. The fast beat charged him and gave an edge to the atmosphere. Tag got up slowly, intending to hurry her outside as fast as possible.

But a tall man in a Stetson stomped through the door, assessed the crowd's response to Claire and circled her shoulder with a muscled, proprietary arm.

North looked fierce enough to give even this wild bunch a run for their money.

North—the man she belonged to.

You cheated, Claire.

A feeling of inevitability thrilled Claire at Tag's volcanic expression when North put his hands on her.

"Let's go, Claire," North said.

She shook him off and rushed deeper into the bar, choosing a table as far from the door as possible. North caught her. He yanked back his chair so fast he nearly knocked their table over.

"What's gotten into you? You're acting like *her*."

"Who? Melody? You don't even see me."

"Well, you've sure got the attention of every other man in this room! Their tongues are mopping the floor."

"Maybe I need a little admiration."

Their waitress arrived. North seethed. Claire ordered two beers.

The door opened again, and a slim figure slipped inside. North shot halfway out of his seat and then fell back heavily. "What's *she* doing here?"

Passion! Livid, pure passion vibrated in North's molten, dark tone now. But he wasn't looking at her.

Melody had captured the spotlight, captured North's full attention. Again, Melody wore tight black jeans and that silky white blouse that caressed her breasts.

When she oozed by him, North sprang out of his chair again.

Slim hips undulating, Melody walked past him without

so much as a glance. Shrimpers hooted. Her smile was sexy, but for the most part, she ignored them all and headed straight for Tag.

Not Tag.

Please, not Tag.

It never took Melody long to steal her friends.

Sure enough, in the next breath Melody was leaning over him. Her arm had wound around his waist, and she was whispering in his ear. With that white grin that lit a fire in Claire's heart and made her eyes sting, he signaled the guy by the jukebox. In the next instant North's favorite song, the same husky melody Melody had danced to at the party filled the room.

Blushing and grinning, Melody broke into her madcap routine. Inspired, she raised her hands above her head and began that same quirky dance that had left North so cold.

But Melody wasn't dancing for North. She was strutting to the music like a rock star on stage. Tag leaned back in his chair like a sultan watching a favorite harem girl. With an appreciative grin, Tag egged her on with suggestive comments. Meanwhile, the shrimpers were stomping and clapping.

Shock filled Claire's throat with a salty taste. She couldn't bear watching her sister captivate Tag as all her special friends had been captivated.

The music got louder. "Get her!" a man said.

Claire heard North's snarled curse.

Melody's terrified cry cut the brittle air.

North sprang out of his chair and shoved the big man who'd grabbed Melody out of the way.

"Don't you dare touch her, you bastard!"

Then he had Melody in his arms, Melody who was protesting every step of the way as he half-dragged, half-carried her from the bar, leaving Claire inside alone.

Claire rose dizzily to her feet. She had to get out of here.

"Claire!" said a husky voice behind her.

Tag's heavy hand fell on her shoulder, spun her around. His haunted, silver eyes burned through her to the bone. Then she remembered Melody and the way he'd looked at her sister. Claire backed away from him in confusion.

"I didn't think you'd come," he said.

"What about Melody? What am I—your consolation prize?"

"No. I asked her to dance for me the way she had for North—to get to you."

Everything but his stark, dark face blurred.

"That was a low-down, dirty trick you pulled," she choked.

"It was so rotten, I thought it might work," he replied tenderly.

As usual his slow, irreverent grin worked a spell. It was crazy. But somehow she believed him.

"You want to dance?" he whispered.

She nodded. "Why not?"

He shot the shrimpers a look that made them turn back to the bar, resume their conversations. His glare toward the pool tables caused a mad scramble for pool cues. Balls began to fly. Somebody put on a slow song as Tag pulled Claire close.

Snugged against his powerful body, she put one hand around his neck. He brought the other to his warm lips in a sweet, loving gesture. Her response was so involuntary she shut out everything except him. It was as if he and she were the only man and woman on earth. As if she'd come home.

He released his hold a little, dancing with her as if she were a virgin at her first prom and he her shy, awed date. "I'm glad you came, Claire." His expression was infinitely gentle.

She hadn't expected to dance like this, to dance sweetly,

tenderly in her wild red dress in this wild, bad place. She
had come looking for something else. Maybe he had, too.
She had thought to prove he was bad. To prove that only
the bad in her could want him.

But he was both passion and tenderness. He made her
feel as pure and cared for as he had that other night when
she'd been so scared. Her fears and jealousies dissolved.
She felt loved and cherished.

He was more than she'd bargained for. As she was for
him. Not that she was ready to accept this truth.

She pressed her head against his chest, heard his heart.

He caught his breath and laughed a little. "I never
thought I'd find anything like this...in a place like
Shorty's."

Neither had she.

Then the door swung open. North loomed in the doorway, his black eyes bleak and dark, his expression harsh.

"You coming home with me, Claire?"

A flutter of panic went through her when she heard the
finality in his voice.

"I have to go," she whispered.

"You have to choose," Tag said, tightening his grip on
her. "Me or him." His gaze seared her.

"I want you. You proved that. But that doesn't change
this. I have to go home with him tonight."

"Choose."

When he saw she already had, Tag's hands fell. His
whole body was tense and coiled. Not so much as a muscle
in his dark face flickered. "A lot of doors have slammed
in my face. If you go, we're done for."

North hurled himself back outside. Without knowing
what she did, she flew after him.

Tag felt the door slam behind her in every cell in his
being. He sank down into a chair, his face as still and white
as bleached stone. He ordered a beer and stared at the door.

"You're losing your touch, Campbell," the bartender said.

Everybody laughed.

Not that Tag gave a damn. Another door had slammed in his face.

Claire was gone.

He'd offered his heart to her, and she'd turned him down flat.

Several beers later, the crowd had begun to thin.

Tag studied the handful of men playing pool. Shrimpers. Men who hadn't had much school. Stubborn men who didn't like to be pushed around. Tag respected these men, but—

But he wasn't one of them. He had a college education. This life, their life—wasn't enough.

There was nothing wrong with being a shrimper. But the life fit men like Frenchy, not Tag. It wasn't his game. Running Frenchy's little empire couldn't thrill him. Not with his experience. Once he'd invested millions of dollars, his father's money, other people's money, and his own.

He belonged in a fancy office. He'd been an investment banker, buying risky businesses, turning them around and then selling them. He'd dealt in big numbers, the same way his father had. He'd been an expert on all kinds of real estate and businesses, all over the country. He'd been a developer, too. There were fat bank accounts in New Orleans that still had his name on them.

He had to go back.

He had to face his father and everything else he'd run from.

"Feeling lonesome?" purred the blonde who'd hit on him earlier. Again, her face blurred. All he saw was golden hair and her tight red dress.

Damn, he wanted Claire.

He'd spent long nights dreaming of her. His body still

ached from their dance. He smiled slowly. "You parked outside?"

Her car was at the edge of the lot, almost hidden in the shadows. When he opened her door, she threw her arms around him, but her slow, hot kisses left him cold.

He hungered for something else entirely—for sweetness, not experience.

For love.

Not this cheap imitation.

For Claire.

This woman tasted of beer and cigarettes and too many other men. Suddenly he felt sick to his stomach.

"Sorry," he said, pulling away.

"Sorry?" She began to laugh. "I'm the one who's sorry. Sorry for wasting my time on a pathetic joke like you. *She* doesn't want you. She thinks you're trash."

"Maybe. But she made me want to be a better man."

She slid inside her car and slammed her door. "A better man? Ha! You're a loser."

Tag stepped into the shadows and watched her drive away.

That's when he saw Claire in North's car.

Eleven

North's arms were folded across the steering wheel. The windows were down. Salty air and the music drifting out of Shorty's filled the car.

"I dreaded telling you this, Claire."

"I'm glad we finally talked," she said gently as she slid his large engagement ring over her knuckle.

"You're ambitious, reliable, respectable—"

She cringed. "Respectable?"

"What I'm trying to say is you really ought to be the perfect girl for me." He fingered the ring, held it up to the light so that it winked at them before he slipped it into his pocket.

"You don't love me. Melody was always between us, even when she was gone," Claire said.

"I don't love her either!" he lashed. "She's just a bad habit I can't seem to kick."

"You sure that's all she is?"

"Melody and me?" He laughed harshly. "You think I'm ever going to forget how she came up to me in that church full of our friends and family? How she took off my ring, handed me that big white bouquet like I was a bridesmaid or something. She looked so sad. When I touched her face to try to calm her, she jumped like I'd shot her and said, 'I can't.' Then she hiked her skirts and ran back down that aisle like a high-stepping French dancing girl."

"She cried her heart out later."

"Melody is like some actress, only it's her real life she lives on stage. I'm tired of it."

"You galloped off after her that day. So did everybody else."

"I made one helluva fool of myself." He gritted his teeth. "Nobody ever made me so crazy. I ran till I passed out. When I came to, I was still holding that damn bouquet. She was gone, and everybody was laughing. Everybody but you."

"She sure stirred you up tonight."

"Me and that whole bar full of men. What was she thinking of?"

"Maybe she still loves you."

"So what if she does? Do you think I want a wife like that? She's too wild. I'm too tame."

"Tame? You should have seen yourself carrying her out of Shorty's."

"My family's way too conservative. Melody says I put her in a cage. And that's what I want to do half the time. The other half I want to strangle her."

"You never once looked at me the way you looked at her tonight."

"What would any man do with a woman like that? China, for God's sake. She took a freighter to China! She was the only woman on that ship. Anything could've happened to her."

"And she made that P.I. Daddy sent walk the plank!"

"Don't remind me. I want to forget her."

"Oh, North." Claire hugged him. "Good luck."

"What about your mother? How's she—"

"I'll handle mother."

North started the car. "I'd better get you home."

As he backed down the drive, the door to Shorty's swung open and Tag stepped outside, his arms around a clingy blonde in a dress a size or two too small for her. The woman's hands were all over Tag.

Suddenly Claire couldn't breathe.

"Isn't that the guy you were dancing with?"

A lump thickened in Claire's throat. She couldn't speak. All she could do was watch them glide together toward a sleek dark car in the shadows. Instead of getting in, they began to neck. Mouth to mouth. Body to body. Claire couldn't believe he let that woman kiss him like that.

But she did believe. He'd mentioned others before her. Classy women on the prowl. She'd been a fool to think what they had was so special.

The couple stopped kissing. The woman got into her car and drove away. That's when Tag saw her.

"Take me home, North," she pleaded. "I'm tired. So tired."

For once North read her. "Maybe it's not as bad as you think."

"It's probably worse."

"Then how come she drove off alone?"

His alarm buzzed. The bright glare of a new sun spilled across Tag. Tag blinked. He'd been dreaming of a slender girl, gold spilling down her back. They'd been dancing.

Awake, all he remembered was how hollow he'd felt when she'd run after North and slammed that door.

He flung a muscular brown arm over his eyes.

Whiskers, a plump roll of purring black fur at the foot of his bed, yawned.

God, his head ached. Had he really drunk that much?

He didn't want to get up, face another day without her. A shadow flitted across him.

Then somebody slammed a fist on his alarm button. Tag sprang to a sitting position so fast sheets and a fat black cat went flying.

Ricky Navarro stood frowning at him from a pool of white light near the window.

"Hell, kid! Haven't I told you not to sneak up on me like that?" His thick voice was blurry with sleepy confusion.

Ricky shrugged and then spun his yo-yo in a defiant arc, caught it, and tossed it out again. But for all the flash, his timing was off. "You don't look so hot," Ricky attacked, his mood defensive. "How come you're still asleep?"

"I don't feel so hot."

Ricky stared moodily out the window.

"How come you're not in school?"

The yo-yo spun out furiously, wobbled and went limp at the end of the string like a dead thing. Something was definitely up. Tag grabbed the string and used it to pull the kid closer.

"Hey, fella, what's wrong?"

Ricky wouldn't look at him. "This…this mean guy Terry said something I didn't like. Pushed me down when I was running to the bus. Made the other kids laugh. Then the bus doors slammed and the bus took off. Without me."

"So? What are we going to do about it?"

"I don't like Terry. He's big and white. I don't like school much, either. Everybody's white and rich but me."

"No. Sometimes it just seems that way."

"I feel all alone."

"Hey." He pulled the string, brought Ricky even closer.

"Other kids. They've got problems, too. But I gotta meet this kid, Terry. I'm gonna drive you to school."

"But I'm scared."

"I'm scared, too. Everybody's scared on the inside, kid. It's something we've all got to lick or hide. You might as well start with this Terry."

"You got a Terry?"

"My Terry isn't just one person. It's my whole, messed up life. The kind of life I want. I just lost something I really wanted, or rather somebody I don't deserve 'cause… 'Cause… It's complicated. I've got to go home, go back where I came from, find myself, face something…deal with *my* Terry, I suppose. If I can do that, you can do this."

"Do you really think so?"

"You need to dream big dreams, kid. That's the only way to turn your life around. But it's not enough to dream. You gotta start makin' 'em happen."

"You're not marrying North?" Dee Dee's whisper was ragged.

"No, Mother." Claire's voice broke. "No…"

For once in her life, Dee Dee wasn't doing three things at once. "I feel like I'm dying," she said weakly.

"So do I, Mother. Why don't we sit down…together?"

Dee Dee had just stepped out of the shower. Still dripping, not bothering to dry herself, she stood stiff and still in her white terry cloth bathrobe. "I…I need to make my bed."

"I'm not going to medical school, either. I—I was just doing that to please you and Daddy."

Blood pounded in Claire's temples. The room felt stuffy. "I don't believe this."

"It's time I figured out who I am, what I want."

"Way past time, Claire." Dee Dee dropped the quilted

coverlet and sank back down onto her bed. "The wedding is almost here."

"I thought I made it clear. North broke up with me last night. There isn't going to be any wedding."

"But you two talked to Reverend Bob. We all did," Dee Dee said disbelievingly.

Claire shook her head in despair.

"What will everybody say?" Dee Dee asked quietly.

"Tell them I'm sorry, or that it's better we found out now...."

"Better? I'll never be able to hold my head up in this town again. Better? This is all your fault." She pressed her hands against her head. Something ugly flickered in her expression. Her pretty mouth thinned. "It's because of *him*, isn't it?"

"I don't know what you're talking about."

"Don't start lying now. No wedding. No medical school. Next, you'll tell me you're in love with that drunk shrimper and that you're going to move into some trashy trailer with him."

"Tag. His name's Tag Campbell. And...and... He wasn't drunk, Mother."

"I know cheap gin when I smell it! He reeked!"

"He poured a whole bottle on himself because he was mad at me."

"What kind of lout would even think up a trick like that?"

"And...and he doesn't live in a trailer. Not that I'd care if he did. He has a beach house."

"You've been there—"

"I...I didn't want to tell you like this...but I—"

"Oh, Claire, you're such a little fool. A man like that, a man who doesn't even bathe—"

"Usually, he does. He's a hard worker and he gets dirty."

Dee Dee's unsmiling mouth hung ajar as she looked up at her daughter. "And how would you know his habits? Oh, God— Rough men like that only want one thing from a young girl like you. He probably thinks you're rich. Oh…. You've been too sheltered. You have no idea. Tell me you haven't slept with him—"

Claire's face caught fire. She ducked her head, so her mother wouldn't see.

"Oh… Oh…. He forced you then? We'll hire lawyers. No. No. Then everybody, all my friends would— We'll—"

Claire swallowed.

Dee Dee buried her head in her hands. "I don't believe this. This is a nightmare."

"Did you ever love Daddy?"

"That's a ridiculous question."

"Is it? Did you just marry him for…"

"What?" Dee Dee pressed her fingertips to her forehead. "How dare you insult *me?* Don't you dare compare my marriage, my life, to the mess you're making of yours. Oh, my head. My aching head. I thought you were different. Not like Melody. I was so proud of you. You were my easy, perfect daughter." She lay down slowly. "Pull the shades." Her voice was weak, fading. "The sun is making my head worse. I—I can feel one of my heat headaches coming on."

"I—If it makes you feel any better, Mother, the shrimper is through with me, too."

"Thank God." Dee Dee pulled a coverlet up to her chin. "Now…now go."

It was nearly eleven o'clock before Tag roared home on his bike. The session in the principal's office had gone well. Like all bullies, Terry was more chicken than tough guy.

Inside his beach house, Tag felt almost as scared as

Ricky when he sat down by his bed and picked up the phone.

Claire. The last time he'd seen her, she'd watched another woman kiss him.

He had to call her. Just on the faint chance…he'd been wrong about her and she would listen to his explanation. He set the phone down, lifted it again, at least half a dozen times. But every time he punched out her number, he got all sweaty, same as that bully Terry had under fire.

What the hell was he so scared of?

He punched the numbers again.

"Hel-lo," a woman said, as if from a deep well.

"Is Claire there?"

"Who is this?" The pained voice perked up a little.

"I said I want to speak to Claire."

"I won't get her unless I can say who is calling."

"Tag Campbell."

"You!" Dee Dee's voice screeched. "She just told me you two were through! Leave her alone. She's a young, innocent girl. A man like you can offer her nothing but trouble. Do we understand each other?"

"You said if I told you who I was you'd get her, Mrs. Woods."

"I lied." She hung up.

He slammed the phone down. Then he sat hunched over in silence for a long while, fuming, brooding.

To hell with Claire and her mother. Claire wanted North, her nice safe life, and there wasn't a damn thing he could do about it.

With grim dread he picked up the phone again. This time he called his father.

The old man took his time coming to the phone. He didn't sound much like himself either. His voice was thin, thready, far weaker than Dee Dee's had been when she'd first answered.

"You're alive," the old man whispered. "Thank God." There was a long incredulous, joyous silence. "I thought— You don't give a damn what I thought. Just come home— son."

Son.

The word resonated inside Tag long after his father spoke it. There was a labored pause.

"We have a lot to talk over," continued his father. "I'm afraid there's not much time."

Melody was throwing tangles of clothes into a huge purple duffel bag that had big yellow butterflies all over it.

"Where are you going this time?" Claire asked.

"I know somebody in India." Melody's voice was brittle.

Melody had friends everywhere.

"What about North?"

Melody's pain-filled eyes locked on hers for a brief moment. Then she grabbed a pair of her thong panties defiantly. "You sure you don't want these?"

Claire shook her head. "You and he—"

Melody looked down. With shaking hands she began to fold a blouse. "He made it very clear in the parking lot last night that he hates me."

"Did he kiss you?"

"Such a kiss. I think he hates me. Really hates me. My lips and arms are still bruised. He said awful, awful things. Every time I think about—"

"He broke up with me. He loves you."

"Whatever he feels, he makes me feel awful. Trapped. Why did I ever like him so much? I don't want to ever see that stuffy, bossy, impossible individual again. He had no right to...to...to hold me against that wall and...overpower me."

"North did that? Your little dance must've—"

"I don't want to talk about it." Melody drew a deep, indignant breath. "So…you and Tag—"

"He left Shorty's with another woman."

"Maybe you didn't see what you think you saw."

"He kissed her."

"Maybe it wasn't like you thought."

"You give him the benefit of the doubt, but not North."

"When a man isn't your guy, you can see clearly. Tag loves you. He's good for you, too. You're not just going through the paces, living somebody else's programmed life. Dee Dee's programmed life." She picked up another pair of thong bikinis. "Trust me. I'm your sister."

They fell into one another's arms, but quickly grew embarrassed and let each other go.

"I don't want you to leave."

"I'll be back," Melody said.

"When?"

"When I feel like it."

Twelve

The shrimper had called, for God's sake.

Dee Dee lay in the dark. If only she could sleep. But her head throbbed, and her heart ached.

Children. Daughters. Maybe Sam had been right to want sons so much.

None of her grand plans for the girls had panned out. How did other mothers raise children who did what they were supposed to do? She was chewing on this puzzling problem when she heard Sam's diesel Mercedes chug up their drive.

Dear God. What was he doing home at this hour? She had no time for him right now. He would fuss about something trivial that had gone wrong at the office. Some patient threatening to sue him, a case gone wrong, or a diagnosis he was clueless about. Worse, he might be hungry. If she didn't fix him something, he'd cook, and the kitchen would look like he'd set off a bomb.

He stomped through the front door, yelling her name. "Dee! Where the hell are my golf clubs? Dee?"

She pressed her temples. Why couldn't he ever find anything?

When she didn't answer, his footsteps trudged up the stairs. The bedroom door was thrown open. He flipped switches. Lights blazed.

He was so thoughtless. She was dying. Not that he who lavished sympathy for a living on strangers, would care.

Even from under her pillow she could hear him rummaging through one of his drawers in that maddening way of his, rooting out mismatched socks, underwear like a giant hamster on the warpath. As usual he dumped an entire drawer onto the floor.

She groaned.

His bulky torso whirled. His quick smile was both thrilled and surprised.

She frowned at the paper cup he'd set on their chest of drawers.

"Why didn't you answer? Why are you in bed?" he demanded, his tone miffed.

She rose, dragged her robe around her aching body, and went to him. "You barge in here, and in the space of one minute, you've turned this side of the room into a garbage bin. And what is that—" She jabbed a manicured nail at his cup.

"My milkshake, damn it!"

She snatched it off the wood. "You're on a diet! You're supposed to snack on that vegetable soup in the fridge I made just for you."

"If I eat one more veggie, I'll become a celery stalk."

She began to cry. Baffled, his arms came around her. The robe slipped off one shoulder, exposing bare skin, and suddenly he got interested, albeit, not in her tears. With a groan, he drew her close, kissing her gently and then not so gently.

"Why are you home?" she whispered, pushing him away.

"It's Wednesday, my afternoon off. I was going to play golf. I was going to dress, find my clubs…but…this is way more interesting."

"This?"

He winked. *"Us."*

Sex was the last thing she wanted, but suddenly, she didn't want him to go.

"Claire's not getting married," she whispered.

"North told me." He kissed her forehead.

"I'm not in the mood," she said stiffly, turning away from him.

"When did that ever stop us?"

"Not now, Sam."

He pulled the robe off. "You look so damn sexy."

"You can't be serious."

"I know how to get that way." He laughed. "Sex at our age is sort of like turning all the lights on the Christmas tree on, but one at a time."

He knew if he pressed her, she wouldn't say no.

He was out the door, back in a jiffy with a bottle of wine, two glasses and a dangerous gleam in his eye. He unlocked a drawer, pulled out a video and handed her her naughty book that had that well-thumbed scene about a virgin being captured by two pirates that shamed her but made her shiver.

It was a ritual. They both knew the moves.

Soon they lay beside each other, sipping wine. She read; he watched his video. Their hands drifted languidly over each other. It wasn't long before quite a few of the lights on their "Christmas tree" began to glow.

Their gazes locked.

She snapped her book shut.

He aimed the remote at the television set, and the screen darkened.

They began to kiss. Ten minutes before she'd had a headache. Now it was gone.

Dark passion drew them out of themselves. They did it twice. On the bed. Then the floor.

When it was over, Dee Dee lay in the crook of his arm, her impossible girls forgotten.

"Sex is so weird," she said.

"I remember how every guy in town wanted you. Hell, you just get better and better."

"So do you," she whispered.

Sam had started out on the wrong side of the tracks. But he'd been smart and ambitious. His wildness had secretly appealed to her.

He got out of bed. "Dee, have you seen my golf clubs? They aren't in the hall—"

She smiled indulgently. "Yes, dear. They're in your trunk."

"The girls will be fine," he promised reassuringly on his way out.

But she didn't want to think about the girls or the wildness in them that made them so impossibly difficult or wonder where they'd gotten it. Instead she fell asleep with a smile on her lips.

Claire didn't drive all the way up to the beach house at the end of the drive off Fulton Road. She got out of the car and studied the charming house tucked under the protective oak trees that the wind had bent and twisted. The swallows that nested under the eaves were riding the wind, soaring up into bright blue and then diving back into their nests. Cats and dogs lay curled in lazy heaps all over his front porch. High grasses waved like shoots of gold beneath a slanting sun. Tag's bike was chained in a shed out back. His boat was tied at the dock. Yet somehow the place wore an abandoned air. As she did. The windows were shut, the storm shutters closed.

Even before she knocked, she knew he was gone and wasn't coming back. Still, she rapped against the screen door till her heart beat against her ribs and her knuckles ached.

Hollow with disappointment, she went around back and let herself inside the breezeway. There she sat, remembering the magic of their first night. An hour passed, and she laid her head wearily against a weathered wall. Soon she was asleep. Which was why she didn't hear the boy until his yo-yo slammed against the wall behind her head.

She jumped.

"Oops!" he said. "Sorry."

He was thin as a wire and as dark as mahogany and too adorably shy to look up from the green yo-yo that he was deftly rewinding with long, agile fingers.

"I'm Claire."

"Ricky." His tone was muffled. "I feed Tag's animals."

"He's gone?"

"New Orleans."

She flinched. "So far?"

"His father was real sick. So he left in a hurry."

"I didn't realize he had a father."

"He don't."

"What?"

"Not no more anyhow. He called this morning. Said he died. Said there's a lot to do there. Said he ain't ever coming back."

"But—" The word was torn out of her. "His house—"

"He's got people here to take care of his stuff. Me."

Desperation was closing over her. "Do you have a phone number? An address?"

"Sure I do. Only I ain't 'sposed to give it to no stranger. You aren't his friend. I know about you. I seen you come out of his house that morning. You were crying. Then you sent that man that tore up his house."

"No, I didn't," she whispered.

"Then who did?"

"It's a long story," she began wearily.

"I got time."

Grief washed Tag in its dark wave. The drapes in his father's office were drawn, so he couldn't see the sluggish curl of the Mississippi beneath him. Tag sat in the shadows, his fists knotted on the massive mahogany desk. All he saw was his father, small and thin, a shadow of the man he'd remembered. How still and white he'd lain against the stiff satin in his coffin.

His huge, indomitable father—gone.

He should've come home a long time ago. His father was dead because he'd passed judgment too readily. Blinded by rage and self-pity and fear, too damn stubborn and insecure to think he might be wrong, he'd hated the wrong man.

Guilt and anguished heartbreak spread through Tag. Had the two of them been put on earth just to hurt each other? He'd gotten off to a bad start with his mother, his aunts, and then his father. Was he doomed to always fail at relationships that mattered? Maybe he should quit trying. Maybe he should stick to what he knew—making money.

His gaze wandered about the room. Damn. His father's presence spoke in every item in his hushed office. The priceless oil and magna on canvas by one of the world's leading painters had been his dad's favorite. But it was the insignificant sculpture of stainless steel that really grabbed Tag's heart and shook him. His father hadn't liked the piece that much, but it had been Tag's first expensive gift to him.

Now the sculpture stood in a pool of light in the center of the room.

Had his father really loved him as he'd professed on his deathbed, grieved over his loss, regretted their quarrel as much as, no, maybe far more than Tag had?

I was wrong about you. It was Hugh. Who would've thought the lazy bastard was smart enough or had it in him?

Hugh, a minor partner, had stolen everything, cheated their clients, tarnished their company's name, cost them millions in lawsuits. Realizing father and son didn't quite trust one another, Hugh had covered his tracks in such a way as to make it look like only Tag or his father could have done it, hoping they would blame each other. When Tag had discovered something was wrong, accused his father and been thrown out, Hugh had sent those goons to finish him. When Tag had vanished, the goons had reported him dead. Hugh must've thought he was home free. But somehow he'd overplayed his hand. His father, never one to trust easily, had set a trap. Then Hugh had run. He'd been caught in Switzerland with very little of the stolen fortune, most of it having been squandered in bad deals.

You were gone. I thought you were dead. It was too late. I couldn't take back the things I said.

I should've stood up for myself. I should've fought too. I was too quick to believe the worst about you.

They had held one another quietly. His father had expired in his arms. The old man had let out that final breath and then had seemed to shrivel like a balloon losing the last of its air. Tag had gone on holding him for a while.

So many lost years.

So much regret. On both sides.

Broken in spirit, his father had never recovered financially. His father had needed him, had searched for him, had become too ill to work as hard as before.

The business wasn't what it had been. Tag was going to have to work very hard.

Funny, how his life had changed instantly, irrevocably. He'd been exonerated and he was rich. His father had left him everything. Only his name wasn't Tag Campbell. It was Scott Duval.

But what did it mean now with his father dead?

It meant everything. Yes, he was grieving. Yes, there was loss. But he had his good name, money, the opportunity to start over, to prove himself. Strangely, those last few precious hours with his father at the end were his most prized legacy.

He had everything he'd ever wanted and more.

Everything except—

His mouth hardened. Forget her.

Nobody could stop him now.

Never again would people slam doors in his face.

Never would women want him just for sex. The Dee Dee's of the world were already telling their ambitious daughters he was quite a catch. Several had been by to check him out. They'd brought cakes, cookies, flowers, notes of sympathy.

To hell with them. He was through with such women and their games. They hadn't ever believed in him. Now he didn't believe in them.

In this mood of bitter grief and triumph, Miriam, his father's secretary, no, *his* secretary now, marched audaciously through the heavy doors.

"I told you to hold my calls, cancel my appointments and leave me alone."

"But there's someone here to see you, sir," Miriam said quietly. "*She* says she's a friend. She doesn't have an appointment."

Miriam was thin and small, but she was no pushover. Her soft voice, sweet smile and impeccable manners con-

cealed a determined will. Tag would put her up against a
dozen tanks any day.

*So, another pretty little jackal was here to get her licks
in when he was at his most vulnerable.*

"I don't have any women friends. I don't have time. Not
with the funeral…"

"But Miss Woods says she knows you from Texas.
She's come all this way to offer her condolences. She's
different from…the others."

"Miss Woods?"

His heart clamored with a wild hurt and white-hot rage
at his complete vulnerability.

Claire, his angel riding the wind.

Claire, who'd slept with him but hadn't given him her
name. Claire, who'd wanted to forget him and marry
money. Claire, who'd chased another man out of Shorty's
and slammed that door in his face.

"She sure as hell didn't waste time." Tag's voice tightened in an effort to leash his emotions. "You tell that witch
to go back where she came from. I never want to see her
again."

Miriam stiffened. "You're making a mistake."

"I'll be the judge of that." He stared her down.

Big-eyed with outrage, she withdrew. "Very well, *sir.*"
When she closed the doors a little too loudly, the purple
shadows swallowed him.

He didn't bother to look up when a metal latch clicked
and a wedge of bright light spilled across the immense
room.

"You're not getting rid of me that easy," said a muted
voice across the darkness.

A wary prickling ran the length of his spine.

"Get out," he lashed.

"I'm sorry about your father," she persisted in that soft,
sweet voice that shredded his heart.

She stepped into the light. Golden hair spilled to her shoulders. Her eyes were the deepest, darkest shade of blue and yet luminous with shimmering passion. God, why did she have to be so damn beautiful?

He let out a harsh, ragged breath. "Who the hell do you think you're kidding?"

Like a vulture she had seized on this vulnerable moment when he felt lost and alone. Seized on the fact that he would take one look at those moist ruby lips, at her, and want her.

She was right. All his pent-up longings seemed to burst inside him. How many nights had he dreamed of her? One look into those eyes, at that incandescent face, and he felt he would die if he couldn't have her again.

When she stood her ground, he got up and strode across the room. Brutally, he yanked her into his arms. "You gambled I'd want this too much, that I'd remember how it was that night...."

"*Us,*" she whispered, her tone strangled.

"Don't!"

He wound his hands in her hair, turned her face up to his, held her near, so near their lips nearly touched, so near her warm breath fell against his mouth. A rush of desire thrummed in his blood.

He loved her.

"You're just here 'cause I'm rich now. You think I'm weak because my father just died. You're worse than all those other women who came on to me in Shorty's."

The shock of his words leveled her like a blow. She went white. Her eyes glazed with pain. So much stark pain. Her knees buckled, but when she started sinking to the floor, his grip tightened. She gave a broken cry and tried to jerk away, but he held her fast.

Damn her. He loved her. He wanted to go home every night and find her there. He wanted to sleep with her, to wake in the dark and know she was there, alive and warm in his bed. He wanted to make love to her, to enjoy the simple pleasures of living with her, his woman, to watch sunsets together and moonrises together. To have children with golden hair and eager bright blue eyes.

Her perfume alone drove him crazy.

"You're just here because you found out I'm even richer than your fiancé," he accused again.

"No…" Her whisper died away in the shadows.

"You didn't want me when you thought I was nothing."

"I did. But…" She swallowed. "Oh, Tag, I'm so sorry. I see now it's too late for us. You've turned cold, set your will against me. You're too prejudiced to listen. I was wrong…then…and so wrong to come here now. But you're wrong, too. I would give anything not to remember you like this. Have you ever…in your whole life…made a mistake about someone…and regretted it?"

"You're good," he snarled. "But why are you really here then? Did your rich, boring cowboy figure out he's really in love with Melody and dump you? Did you come here to save your crushed ego?"

A hot guilty flush climbed her throat, but the color faded long before it reached her pale cheeks. "I'll go."

He yanked her closer. "So, that's it. Well, for your information, I don't want North Black's leftovers. Not for keeps anyway." He felt wild with love for her but dark and lost because she couldn't feel the same. He had to end this. He wanted all or nothing. "I'll give you the name of my favorite bar. It's classier than Shorty's." He scribbled the name on a card and pressed it into her hand. "Drop by tonight if you're still in town, if you've still got the hots for me. I'll play pirate or whatever other fantasy you want to indulge in. Come every night if you like. I want you in bed, but nowhere else."

"Don't," she pleaded. "*I came because I love you.*

And...and, oh, I don't know why I'm telling you that...when it's over.''

"Shut up!" His voice was achingly hard.

"There's nothing I can say to make you believe me. You're so cold, so remote. It's no use. You've made up your mind. You're not going to believe me. I was wrong, Tag, not to see the truth sooner. But I see it now. I love you. I love you poor or rich. I love you even when you're like this.''

Her blue eyes sparkled with tears.

A tight band closed around his chest. Every breath cut like a knife. She was killing him with her beauty and softness.

Her choked voice was almost inaudible now. "I don't blame you for not believing me.''

She turned and ran.

Thirteen

The sky was a dark dove-gray. A thickness hovered over the tight little crowd clustered around Tag who sniffled as he stood at his father's grave. A clergyman in black read from the Bible about a man being both good and bad, about a life never being all of either, about the next life being a better one, about the folly of making judgments, about the need to forgive both the living and the dead. But Tag's heart was too choked with grief to make sense of any of it.

His father was gone.

So was Claire.

Inside Tag, his heart and soul had turned to stone.

All he saw was the gleaming wood of the closed coffin upon which lay lush, blood-red roses. All he felt was the end of everything.

True, a willowy blonde held onto the dark, expensive cloth of his well-cut sleeve. The model was being well paid.

She was window decoration, a pretty lie to keep the press happy.

A brutal one, to keep Claire away.

When the preacher finished, it began to rain. Everybody scurried back to their cars except Tag. While rain pattered on vinyl, he hunkered under the tent and stared gloomily at the coffin.

Tomorrow he would work.

Today he would grieve.

Tears filled his eyes. Or was it only a few stray raindrops hitting his face? After a while the downpour slowed. He wiped his eyes just as a yellow taxi drove through the far gate.

He got up and went to the coffin, picked a red rose from the spray, and turned to go.

The sun came out and a wisp of sunshine caught a slim girl as she got out of the taxi and ran through the drizzle toward him.

Claire. Looking even more scared now than she had that first night on the edge of that other cemetery.

He straightened, threw the rose to the ground, crushed it into the wet grasses with his polished, black shoe.

Slowly, she walked toward him.

"Will you be all right?" she whispered.

As if she cared.

He nodded, touched beyond words by her presence. His face frozen into an icy mask.

She reached a hand toward him, and he wanted her touch more than anything even though he knew he would be lost then. But the willowy model had precise instructions. The sum he was paying for her performance was generous.

The door of the long white limo opened, and the beautiful girl spoke silkily, sexily. "Are you coming—darling?"

Anguish ripped his heart, but he forced a slow, dazzling smile, his bedroom smile.

Claire stared from the girl to him wordlessly, and then her stark face drove a final nail through his chest. Claire's coming here meant too much when he felt so lost and alone. This had to be a deliberate, calculated act on her part. And yet her white face looked as grief-stricken as he felt.

"I'm glad you came, Claire," he muttered. The rough, honest words were torn from him.

She didn't hear the love in his voice or see the tumult of emotion in his tortured eyes because she was already running through the wet green grass.

Then he was running after her, his long strides stalking her.

She got in the cab and sped away.

"Claire!"

Thunder crashed; the sky turned black. It started to pour again. He raced after her till his custom-made suit was soaked, his Italian shoes ruined and his heart pounding so hard he thought it would explode.

Still panting, he collapsed inside his limo beside the model a few minutes later.

"Did I do okay?" she asked worriedly.

Rain dripped through his long black hair, down his face in cold rivulets. He was shaking so hard all he could do was nod.

The model smiled.

He sank against rich black leather. "Turn on the heater," he ordered the driver. "Take us home."

Claire was gone for good.

Tag told himself it was for the best.

Tag didn't like reporters much. This one was cute though, with her red hair and bright blue eyes.

Blue eyes.

Forget *her.*

The reporter was young, a little shy, and too easily impressed. Which made the interview more fun.

Ads were expensive. Articles about his projects cost nothing and were far more readily believed.

"From rags to riches," she gushed. "Wow! Nobody in this city can stop talking about you, Mr. Duval. You've only been back two months—"

"Two and a half," he corrected in a hard voice. *Seventy-seven days, four hours.*

It felt like a lifetime since he'd seen Claire.

Forget her.

"How does it feel—to have the best of everything?"

"I'd rather talk about my projects—"

"All those beautiful women, your yacht, plane. Mr. Duval, you certainly live the fantasy life."

Fantasy. He could tell her a thing or two about fantasy.

"Do I?" he murmured.

Strip, my lady. Slowly.

He saw a slim girl winding silk around herself and a pirate holding her close in a moondark bay.

"You have it all, Mr. Duval. Everything a man could possibly want. We'll want to get shots of your house, your buildings, of you out on a date or two with women, your yacht...."

He got up, went to the long window and stared out at the cranes above Duval Towers. He'd granted this interview to publicize that project.

Success. He had it in spades. He had everything he'd ever wanted.

So, why was he counting the days, the hours?

And the nights? Oh, the nights. When he slept he fantazied about ruby lips, pink-tipped breasts and golden hair. He woke every hour, feeling hot and tight, ready to explode.

And every waking hour he remembered her white, grief-stricken face when he'd smiled at the model in the cemetery.

Why was life so hard without her?

Claire stared at the pictures of Scott Duval and the willowy model. His picture brought both pain as well as the shock of physical arousal.

So, he was still dating that same girl. She was in every picture. Claire devoured the celebrity issue of the magazine that had done a lengthy profile on him.

Did Tag…Scott ever even think of her?

Almost, almost, she felt desperate enough to run back to New Orleans. She still remembered the name of that bar. But the cost of such a night, if he still wanted her that way, knowing she loved him, would be too much to bear.

The summer had been slow and hot—endless. Loverboy never taunted her now. She'd stopped talking to herself in the mirror, stopped dreaming.

Maybe that meant she'd grown up at last. She'd been interviewing for teaching jobs in the fall. She didn't know what she wanted to do with her life. She couldn't really think when the days were so long and hot, when her future seemed to stretch before her endlessly, without meaning. But she had to do something.

"You've got to think about your future," Dee Dee was always pressuring.

"That's hard, knowing I threw away the one thing I can't live without."

"Life goes on, Claire."

"Have you ever been in love, Mother? Really, madly, passionately in love?"

"You know how much I love your father."

But she didn't. "That's not what I mean, Mother."

"Young love…is only the beginning." Her mother

picked up the magazine, flipped through the pictures that so tormented Claire. "I was wrong about Tag. About you. Will you ever forgive me?"

"Oh, yes. If I've learned anything out of this, it's to forgive."

If only he could have forgiven her.

Fanta-Sea's shrouds sang as Claire furiously scrubbed brightwork that didn't need polishing.

Nothing mattered to her now. The summer was nearly over. Two principals, one in Orange, the other in El Paso, towns at opposite ends of Texas, each colorful locales, had offered her jobs. But she didn't want either one.

"What you want, you can't have."

Go home. It's getting too dark to see.

But when she set her rag down and went below, a low wolf whistle made her spine tingle.

Startled, she whirled.

Nobody was there, so she enjoyed the last of the light fading from the magenta sky as well as the lap of purple wavelets.

She remembered another night. Another boat.

Don't remember him.

A shadow fell across her.

"Strip, my lady. Slowly," said a husky voice.

"Don't tease me, Loverboy," she pleaded. "Not now."

Still thinking it was only her imagination, she whirled.

Fierce silver eyes burned to her soul. Or, rather one very irreverent eye. The other was hidden by a black satin patch.

Excitement pierced her like an electric shock. She made an incoherent little cry when she saw the tall figure in a flowing white shirt and tight black jeans. Again, he was dressed like a pirate. Only this costume was sexier. He stood with his legs set widely apart, an earring sparked from the dark.

Lean and bronze, too unholy and wild for words, shadows dominating his dusky bone structure, her midnight fantasy had come to life.

"Nice shirt," she whispered, her heart hammering in her throat.

"Strip, my lady." His languid grin lit every part of her. "Slowly."

"You've got to be out of your mind." She felt the thrill of being driven once more by ungovernable impulses and heady emotions.

His voice was tender. "Or maybe I've come to my senses."

"What about that woman…in that fancy magazine?" she croaked. "The blonde?"

"There haven't been any women. Not a single one. No blonde. She was a paid employee. A human scarecrow…to scare you away."

"That's such a ridiculous… But…you're here. And I…I…I'm such a little fool…I believe you."

He climbed down the stairs and picked her up.

"Put me down," she whispered.

But he stomped back up on deck and held her over the side.

"Put me down—now."

"Anything to please a pretty lady." With that same slow grin, he dropped her into the water.

She started to scream and ended on a gurgle of saltwater. Under water, angry bubbles spewed to the surface. Furious, she kicked her way upward.

He was in the water, too. His arms came around her.

"I love you, Claire."

"You ruined my hair."

He pointed to a shrimp boat. "Swim for it," he ordered.

Her arms sliced through the water. She kicked off her shoes and swam quickly. Once on board, inside the pilothouse, he held her so close, his hot body burned her through their wet clothes.

"You're so beautiful," he said. "I don't even have a picture of you."

She traced his stubborn, cleanly-shaved jaw, ran her hands through the heavy black hair glued to his brow. "I...I can't believe you're really here." She began to shiver.

"We've got to get you out of these wet clothes."

Her pulse thrummed. "Kiss me first," she whispered. "Love me...."

"Always. Forever."

"Marry me," she whispered.

"Not so fast. That's my line."

"All right. Go on. Ask me."

"Why? I already know you will."

"You weren't this conceited when you were a shrimper."

"Money does things to people."

"I don't care about the money. I love you. I have never loved anybody else."

"I don't want anybody else but you either," he finally said.

"When I read that article I thought you had everything in the world you ever wanted."

"Not if I don't have you. I don't care where I live, or how much money I make, I want you. You're everything."

"That's exactly how I feel about you."

"Claire, I've been mixed up for a long time. When you didn't choose me at Shorty's, it opened old wounds that are just now beginning to heal. When you came to New Orleans, you were sweet to me, but I wouldn't let myself trust you...or anybody else, for that matter. I don't want to live like that anymore. All the money in the world isn't worth it. I was a jerk to you in my father's office…and at the cemetery. Can you ever forgive me?''

''Of course. Love doesn't hold on to wrongs. I behaved badly, too.''

Then his mouth found hers, and as with all lovers, something more than words was needed. His breath was warm, his arms tight around her waist, his muscular body flooding her with heat but with tenderness too.

Their kiss told them both everything they needed to know, erased all doubts, forgave all wrongs. Most of all it showed them both how much they yearned.

''I love you,'' she said.

His arms wrapped tighter around her waist. Then he pulled her down below to a bed with red silk sheets. But she got up and began to whirl slowly, stripping with an expertise that made his eyes darken with wildness.

''You've been practicing,'' he said appreciatively, a smile curving his mouth.

They kissed. They made love. Wrapped in thin cotton blankets, they shared the sunset. And the sunrise. The first of many, she hoped.

Epilogue

With a shudder the helicopter rose into the sparkling air above the wedding party. Higher and higher, till the golden bride in her swirling veil and her handsome dark groom inside the cockpit soared above the island that winked to them like a pine-covered emerald in an aqua sea.

Their wedding had been written up in all the national magazines. Melody had caught the bouquet, and Dee Dee had been in her element. Sam hadn't minded the third wedding at all even though it was more lavish than the first two he was still paying for. Because the groom had paid for everything.

"Where are we going? I hope it's not far," Claire yelled above the noise of the rotors.

Tag pointed down.

She saw a ship with furled sails at anchor in a cove. White surf lapped against sugary beaches.

The pilot began his descent.

The flutter of a skull and crossbones against black at the top of the highest mast on the ship caught her attention.

Claire clapped her hands and laughed in delight. "Why...why it's a pirate ship."

"I hoped that come midnight, it would inspire you."

"Long before midnight," she teased. "The wedding was perfect. You are perfect. The ship is perfect."

"I love you, darling," he whispered. "More than I can ever say."

And she was inspired long before midnight.

They were below in the lavish captain's quarters.

Alone together.

She smiled. "Strip, my lord. Slowly."

He laughed. "That's my line, Mrs. Duval."

"Mrs. Duval," she repeated the name.

His brown hand found a white satin covered button.

"You were my first virgin. My first bride. My first love. And this is the first wedding dress I ever took off a woman."

"And the last, I hope," she murmured.

"For sure," he agreed.

An amazing sense of completeness filled her as he began undoing the long line of buttons that ran the length of her slim spine.

Happily ever after was no longer a dream but her reality. She had found everything she ever fantasized about and more.

With him.

"I love you," he said.

"Then prove it."

"What do you have in mind?"

"Ravish me. Be my midnight fantasy."

* * * * *

If you enjoyed Ann Major's

MIDNIGHT FANTASY,

you will love her next title

WILD ENOUGH FOR WILLA

From MIRA BOOKS
On sale December 2000
Don't miss it!

For a sample of
WILD ENOUGH FOR WILLA,
turn the page....

Wild impulses. Reckless deeds.

The narrow shelf high above the desert floor upon which Mrs. Willa Longworth perched would have been tricky in broad daylight. In the cool, wet, midnight dark of that November evening, the ledge sheered to nothingness. The chill that raced up her spine had nothing to do with the low temperature.

Four years of marriage to a dying husband hadn't changed Willa Longworth nearly as much as they should have. Or, maybe they had. She felt near bursting inside—for adventure. For life.

Rash actions were her special forte. She wasn't nearly so different from the girl who'd offered herself to the highest bidder that terrible night in Laredo as she wished she was. Not so different from the girl who'd recklessly married a dying man with a fortune.

Tonight, when any other woman would have known all was lost—she'd taken the money. *So...she was a thief now.*

Oh, well.

Willa believed in beauty, in prayer, in spirits, in Gypsy fortune-tellers, in gold at the end of rainbows, in signs from above, in wishes that come true, in all sorts of wondrous concepts that make no sense to logical people.

Despite several regrettable experiences with that dangerous, dashing breed of men Willa foolishly fell for, she still believed in true love. But until the plane crashed just north of her ranch house outside of Taos during the storm earlier tonight, until she found ten briefcases stuffed with fifty-dollar bills inside its wreckage, she'd never received such dramatic proof that her beliefs held merit.

There was a God.

The sisters couldn't drive away her and her young son now.

Neither could that nasty, foul-mouthed Luke McKade, who knew about her past and enjoyed threatening to destroy her.

The briefcases were heavy as lead. There was probably a million dollars in them.

So much money and it was all hers.

Not yet.

Not till she hid these last two briefcases.

Move.

A strange fear paralyzed her. The last two briefcases seemed heavier, the cliff higher. Maybe it was her guilty conscience weighing her down.

She thought of the twisted fuselage. There hadn't been any bodies. That meant the pilot and his passengers were still alive. What if *they* came back?

If she kept the money, she and Sam could stay. She could tear up Hesper's check, act high and mighty like a real lady and announce primly, ''You can't buy me!'' She would send that oversexed McKade packing, too.

Far beneath her, the New Mexican desert slumbered as peacefully as a baby. Not a sound, not even a nightbird or the slither of scales against stone, did she hear. Nothing. Still, she sensed unseen eyes in the darkness and shivered at the thought of Luke McKade. He had a bad habit of turning up when she least wanted him to, of catching her at her worst.

Moonlight silvered the cliffs and the beautiful valley where she and Sam lived. Where they could have been so happy if only...if only the sisters could have accepted them. If only McKade would quit burning a hole through her with his eyes. If only he would quit threatening to expose her. But for reasons he had never divulged, Luke wanted to bed her and send her packing.

Willa forced herself to begin climbing again. A few twists and turns had her panting, but soon she reached that spot where the path seemed to end at a sheer, blank wall. Only, it didn't. One tricky step, a jump into the darkness had her inside the small opening where she'd hidden the other briefcases.

Her stomach tightened as she clicked open each briefcase. Excitedly she ran her flashlight over the clumps of fifty-dollar bills.

She wasn't really a thief. No, this was like Robin Hood. She needed the money badly.

Now she and Sam were free. Respectable.

She grabbed wads of bills, but just as she began stuffing them into the pocket of her jeans, heavy footsteps crunched dry earth outside the entrance.

Tensing with terror, she sprang to her feet.

Pebbles spun. Then there he was, huge and dangerous, trapping her inside the shadowy cave.

McKade. He was tall and dark and, as always, too handsome for her own good. There was that overpowering energy about him, that magnetism that both drew her and frightened her. She quivered as she had that first, terrible night when he'd planted ten crisp hundred-dollar bills in her shaking fingers and she'd so foolishly sold herself to him.

"Finders keepers, *Widow* Longworth," he jeered in that

same silken, deadly voice. His cold smile filled her with dread.

"You!"

He laughed, some of his tension easing at her obvious dismay. "Your worst nightmare."

Their gazes locked.

His silver eyes drifted, devouring her pale face, her breasts.

When she gasped in outrage, his devilish grin broadened.

His unwanted hunger was spiced with guilt and resentment and fear as well as by his own fury that he still found her so attractive. Quickly she averted her eyes to the wall. Just as rapidly he forced his gaze to the money.

"Get out," McKade said. "The money's mine."

The money was everything. Her future. Sam's.

She put her hands on her hips and stayed put.

"I said, 'Get out!' Now!" McKade swaggered toward her, no doubt confident of his superior physical power. Ignoring her, he knelt over the briefcases.

Her briefcases.

When his large brown hands began greedily fingering the money, something snapped in her brain.

She sprang. He caught her by her slim waist and rolled on top of her. Attempting to claw him, she screamed and wept. Patiently he waited till she exhausted herself with too much flailing and too many tears. Only when she stilled against him did he free her hands and wipe away her gritty tears with a callused fingertip.

His finger lingered on her cheek as it had the first time he'd touched her that other horrible night.

"Damn it," he whispered.

His intense gaze heated her skin. With a scowl he yanked his hand away, flushing darkly. As always, he was mad as hell she turned him on. She was extremely shy and unsure about sex, even with him, but suddenly, ancient female intuition took over. He was bigger. But Delilah had bested Samson, hadn't she?

Before she quite realized what he intended, McKade kissed her. Not as hungrily as she would've expected. No, almost gently. So gently and so reverently, he stole her breath away.

She forgot the money. Her quickening heartbeats made her realize she was every bit as low as he was where sex was concerned.

"I don't love you," she said. "I don't even like you."

"Better," he whispered, nibbling her ear with an expertise that alarmed her.

"Better?"

"Better than hate. No telling how your mood will improve once we do it...and the money makes me a rich man."

The money. How could she have forgotten it for one single second?

No man, especially not this conceited, oversexed devil, was going to use and discard her as if she were nothing. *Never again....*

*The Fortune family requests
your presence at the weddings of*

*Silhouette Desire's provocative new miniseries
featuring the beloved Fortune family and
five of your favorite authors.*

Bride of Fortune—August 2000
by Leanne Banks (SD #1311)

Mail-Order Cinderella—September 2000
by Kathryn Jensen (SD #1318)

Fortune's Secret Child—October 2000
by Shawna Delacorte (SD #1324)

Husband—or Enemy?—November 2000
by Caroline Cross (SD #1330)

Groom of Fortune—December 2000
by Peggy Moreland (SD #1336)

*Don't miss these unforgettable romances...
available at your favorite retail outlet.*

Where love comes alive™

COMING NEXT MONTH

#1309 THE RETURN OF ADAMS CADE—BJ James
Man of the Month/Men of Belle Terre
An outcast from his home, Adams Cade had returned to Belle Terre to face his family—and his childhood love, Eden Claibourne. But when their reunion was threatened by Adams' past, could Eden convince him that his true home was in her arms?

#1310 TALLCHIEF: THE HOMECOMING—Cait London
Body & Soul/The Tallchiefs
The discovery of Liam Tallchief's heritage was still raw when sassy Michelle Farrell barreled into his life doing her best to unravel all his secrets. Michelle had never been a woman to stay in one place too long. So when Liam kissed her, why did she feel a fierce urge to claim *him?*

#1311 BRIDE OF FORTUNE—Leanne Banks
Fortune's Children: The Grooms
Accustomed to working with powerful men, Adele O'Neil instinctively knew that it would take a brave woman to get close to larger-than-life Jason Fortune. Could she be that woman? His touch must have jumbled her brain, because she was suddenly dreaming of home and hearth....

#1312 THE LAST SANTINI VIRGIN—Maureen Child
Bachelor Battalion
When Gunnery Sergeant Nick Paretti was ordered by his major to take dance lessons, he never expected his partner to be feisty virgin Gina Santini. And though the sparks flew when they were pressed cheek to cheek, Gina yearned for so much more. Could this gruff marine become Gina's partner—in marriage?

#1313 IN NAME ONLY—Peggy Moreland
Texas Grooms
Preacher's daughter Shelby Cannon needed a father for her unborn child—and rodeo cowboy Troy Jacobs was the perfect candidate. Only problem was, the two would have to be married in-name-only...and Troy was determined to make his temporary bride into his forever wife!

#1314 ONE SNOWBOUND WEEKEND...—Christy Lockhart
There was a snowstorm outside, a warm fire in his house, and Shane Masters's ex-wife was in front of him declaring her love. Shane knew that Angie had amnesia, but as they were trapped together for the weekend, he had only one choice—to invite her in and this time never let her go....

CMN0700